MW01677835

Monet's Garden

Monet's Garden

John Lent

19/03/97
For Chris,
All the best to you, Chris.
Especially in your own
writing. Cheers.
John

Thistledown Press Ltd.

©1996, John Lent
All rights reserved

Canadian Cataloguing in Publication Data

Lent, John

Monet's garden / by John Lent. –

ISBN: 1-895449-56-1

I. Title.

PR9199.3.L444M65 1996 C813'.54 C96-920051-X
PS8573.E58M65 1996

Book design by A.M. Forrie
Cover art by Jude Clarke
Set in 11 pt New Baskerville
by Thistledown Press

Printed and bound in Canada by
Veilleux Printing
Boucherville, Quebec

Thistledown Press Ltd.
633 Main Street
Saskatoon, Saskatchewan
S7H 0J8

Thistledown Press acknowledges the support received for its publishing program from the Saskatchewan Arts Board and the Canada Council's Block Grants program.

This book is for my father, Harry Lent (1922-1991),

and my friend, Jack Schratter (1935-1992).

Acknowledgements

I would like to thank the editors of the following periodicals for publishing earlier versions of these stories in *Dandelion, Event, Grain* and *New Quarterly.*

I would also like to thank Okanagan University College Professional Development Fund and The Banff Centre for giving me the time and resources to work on this manuscript, and especially the following writers for their advice at The Banff Centre in 1993: Edna Alford, Sandra Birdsell, Don Coles, Alistair MacLeod, Rhea Trebegov, Rachel Wyatt and David Zeiroth.

Writing often depends upon people close to me, and each of the following have played a role in the growth of this manuscript: my creative writing students, Al Forrie, Neil Fraser, Nancy Holmes, the Kalamalka New Writers Society, George Larsen, Gary Marfleet, Linda McConnell, Craig McLuckie, Paddy O'Rourke, Jay Ruzesky, Greg Simison, Glen Sorestad, Don Summerhayes, Simone Vauthier, Tom Wayman and, as always, Jude Clarke.

Special thanks to Margit Schratter for continuing a great friendship.

Thanks to everyone at Thistledown Press, and, especially, Seán Virgo.

Contents

Diction - conformity - repetition of the word order, reliable, ritual ceremony.

3rd person Limited omniscient narrator

Past tense - Narrator is reflecting life history.

Rick, Jane, Neill, Father, Mother

Setting - South Side Edmonton Park Ellen area

Dialogue is limited

Theme of volume: Title of 1st chapter to narrator in root sequence

As Far as He Could See

Rick slipped into his blue jacket and walked through the side door of the Sacristy, out into the Church. The Sacristy concealed the secrets of the place, the guts in behind the stage. He was part of those guts now and it gave him a double vision. He could feel all the parts of the ceremony; he assisted in each small gesture that built the whole order of the mass, and he loved this order. He knew exactly what would happen, and when.

There was something in the safety of the repetition that carried him, each morning, away from confusion into a spot where he could rise above it. The second part of the vision had to do with the humanness that produced the order: all the flaws and imperfections that vanished somehow in the playing out of the ritual itself. It fascinated him to see those imperfections bleached into safety, into an order that seemed invincible, irresistible.

He'd been here at the seven o'clock mass every morning for the past year; he'd become one of the most reliable altar boys in the parish. He prided himself on that. Even Father Macleod, infamous for his bad moods, had accepted him.

As he walked past the communion rail to the center aisle, he could hear him hacking away behind the doors. Father Macleod had a terrible cough. All the altar boys were aware of the rumours that he could have played professional football down east in Ontario, but these rumours were tempered by his paunch, the heavy smoking that caused gobs of phlegm to be spit out into his hankie, and his demand for more than the usual drop of wine at the Offertory. Still, he was in charge of the place. There was no doubt about it. When he raised the Eucharist in his hands each morning, when his lips spoke the words, *Hoc est enim corpus meum,* there were no imperfections in the air. They'd been transformed, carried elsewhere somehow. *This is my body,* Rick whispered to the sounds of the hacking.

He knelt down at the communion rail and stared at the tabernacle. He rested his lips on the rail and bit into it softly and tasted the oak. As he leapt up and headed down the center aisle, he was encompassed by the smell of it. He loved the oiled polish of the pews and the fixtures, and tried to hold them as they fell forward like a soft shuffle of yellow cards tumbling on the sides of things as he approached the carved, heavy door. He leaned forward into it and it creaked outwards into the April air waiting down on 62nd Avenue.

The sun was up now, a thin white-gold band strung taut over all the shingled roofs. As he stood on the top of the Church steps, the grey roofs floated away from him like a charcoal sea. So few hills broke the flatness of south Edmonton that the roofs receded like an ocean forever southward, as far as he could see, until the power poles, and finally Cemetery Hill broke the roofs against something else. Like the times his father had taken him out to Mahoney Beach in Nova Scotia before they'd moved west, and as Rick had watched the tide for jellyfish, his father had sat quietly watching him, drinking from the flask tucked into his coat.

He zipped his jacket and felt his shoes click on the cement. His dark brown penny-loafers made him feel so light. After months of Edmonton snow, after the relentless wool and rubber of his defenses against it, he felt he was floating like a feather into the blue spring air. It was incredible, this gift of lightness, and yet it was such a small gift. He was twelve. It was 1960. He had trained himself to rise up over his tiny southside world and stare down at it, and it was true: it was paltry, insignificant. These big moments inside were nothing to the world around him. He knew that. When his heart swelled like this, though, when he felt a perfect, ordered breath around him sometimes, he suspected a connection he couldn't see. So he hesitated on the stairs, trying to keep it all in his head, then dove down into the street where, as usual, he lost the bigness of things and was engulfed by its detail instead.

There were bright yellow crocuses sprouting up in Mr. Turner's lawn in front of the caragana hedge. The hedge itself seemed dry and brittle, lifeless. It was the skeleton of something that used to be alive in the air. A light flicked on, then off in Mr. and Mrs. Deagle's kitchen. Was Donny up yet? It didn't look like it. He could see his basement window from the street and it was still dark in there.

When he turned South at Mrs. Moynton's pine trees, he stared over at the huge orange backhoe sitting lifeless in the yard to the side of the United Church. They were putting in new plumbing and a parking lot there. He'd heard they were going to have the parking lot paved. Why couldn't his own Church afford to do that, too? Father Macleod had spent the last two years raising money for the new pews. The old ones had been folding chairs that were cheap and noisy and always falling apart, but the new were long and silent, graceful, worth it. The parking lot could wait. They only had trouble with dust from the gravel in the summers anyway. It was a small thing compared to the pews. His parents said the city was going to pave all the sideroads in the fall. Maybe they'd pave St. Agnes' parking lot then, too. Maybe then they'd catch up. Maybe then, too, the bus would come down 109th Street as far as the Church instead of stopping at 65th Avenue. That would be nice for Mom. They were so stuck down here, away from the center of the city.

Mrs. Seminiuk was moving around in her kitchen. She carried a bright copper kettle over to the sink from the window. She'd been at Mass, too. Like him, she was always there, but left right after Communion, and was home before eight o'clock. Some of his parents' friends whispered she was a saint, but other people hinted something had happened to her children. Something terrible had left her alone like this. Was she at mass every morning for the same reason he was? Was there something she feared that was bleached away, over and over again, as Father Macleod's lips mouthed those words?

Her window disappeared as he gained 61st Avenue and the sun popped up from behind Mr. and Mrs. Brown's eaves. Across the gravel his parents' house sat, still, in the morning air around it. His dad placed something in the back of the Meteor, slammed the trunk closed, then disappeared past the stucco into the backyard. His dad was wearing a white shirt with the sleeves rolled up to the elbows. He was up early for a Saturday. This was his day off and he often slept in. It was great for Jane and Neil and him when their father slept in because they could slip away before he decided there were projects he wanted done around the house. This could be a bad sign. It was hard to say. The other side of it was that if he was up this early it also meant he wasn't hungover, and he and Mom would be in a good mood. It could go anywhere, he reminded himself, and his heart sped up at the openness of it, the things he couldn't see.

The Saturday before, his dad had slept in. He'd been hungover because of Friday night. There'd been a big fight about money at suppertime. Rick, Jane and Neil had hidden downstairs in the basement, pretending to play. It was a bad fight that ended with their mom sitting in the kitchen, crying, and their dad slamming the door and speeding away in the car. In the middle of the night, the police had brought him home. One of his eyes was bruised because he'd been in a fight with another teacher he didn't like, in the Park Hotel Bar. He'd tried to joke it all away the next night, and they'd tried to joke it away with him.

Rick knew his neighbourhood so well he felt he could see the asphalt roofs from a height, and hear people sleeping or moving around quietly beneath them as he ran down the street. Like he was hovering over it in a helicopter or a plane. The Kidmans lived in the white corner house. They were protestants, and had just moved in before Christmas. The second, green house belonged to the Reimers. They were German and the older boy, Carl, had hanged himself in the garage last summer. Whenever he passed the Reimer house, a shadow fell over the safety Rick wrestled from his world. He wondered again and again about Carl. He'd never had anything to do with Rick or his friends because he was in his late teens. He imagined Carl hanging in the darkness of the garage, his shoes just inches from the chair he'd kicked out beneath himself, while Rick and Neil were playing road hockey in the lane behind the garage, yelling and laughing while Carl died. How could anything get so bad a person would do that? The Reimer house had an aura around it now, of sadness, of fear. Nobody talked about them anymore. There was something else wrong, and Rick couldn't see what it was.

He ran his hand over the back of the Meteor where it sat thick and blue above the gravel. They were the veterans in the neighbourhood now. They'd moved in six years ago, just after the subdivision had been built by the Golden Construction Company. His mother still had the brochures. She loved to bring them out. They made everything seem official, she'd say as she leafed through them in the kitchen.

He laughed to himself as he rounded the back corner of the house and slipped in the door. He could hear his parents' voices chafing against one another at the front of the house, in the living room.

Sometimes his life felt suspended between these voices whispering different things to him. His mother's voice was optimistic, hopeful, talked of success and delighted in all the signs of it in doctors' lives, lawyers' lives, the voices of politicians and priests. Her father had been a jeweller in Moncton and had lost his business in the depression, and her voice contained that loss and sought something to undo it. His father's voice, on the other hand, contained surprises and twists and turns. Mainly, though, it was a voice that mocked things, the things his mother's voice praised, and Rick felt caught between them often. One night in the Church hall after Christmas, the night of their wind-up hockey banquet, Rick and Neil had sat spellbound as their father had held court, making everyone laugh with his funny stories. It seemed incredible how much authority his father's voice held, but he'd disappeared in the end. He'd drunk too much at the banquet, and that's what had fuelled the stories. Mr. Jewell had found their father asleep in the car, and had given them a ride home. His father had to go and pick up the car the next morning and had laughed sheepishly to Neil and Rick about a flu he must have picked up at school.

"It'd be a nice thing to do," she said. "Why don't you take him then?"

"Because," Rick could hear his father sigh back, "It's just one of your hare-brained ideas, Colette. It's not mine."

"That shouldn't make any difference, Charles," she said, more softly now, "It would just give him a chance to spend some time with you."

"Well, why would he want to do that?" his father said.

"Oh, come off it, Charles. He thinks about you all the time. You know that."

"Little goody-two-shoes!" his father laughed, "Those beady little eyes judging me all the time!"

"Who's getting dramatic now?" his mother laughed.

"Well, he's not judging you, though, is he?"

They sat in the darkness of the living room with one small lamp on and the drapes closed against the light.

"Hi!" Rick said. "I'm just going to make some toast. That all right?"

"Sure, dear," his mother replied and followed him out into the kitchen. "Use the brown loaf over there."

She walked over to the kitchen table and sat down near the window with her cup of tea. His father's head loomed into the doorway to the kitchen and stared at him while the bread toasted. Rick couldn't figure out the half smile on his father's face, so he smiled back at him, imitating it.

Usually, when he mimicked him like this, he could make his father laugh, and he loved making him laugh. In his father's case, though, the laughter had something to do with things going wrong, not right. It was the opposite of the mass Rick had just come from. In his father's rituals, the only safety was in leaving imperfections alone, exulting in them. Rick had learned this in his father over time, and though he didn't understand it, he could mimic it to make him laugh. This time, his father didn't laugh. He just kept staring at him, deciding something. "Have your toast," he said finally, breaking the stares. "I've got to go up to McGavin's and the school. Would you like to come with me?"

"Thanks Dad," Rick said. He looked over at his mother who was smiling at him secretly. "You should have heard Father Macleod this morning, Dad."

"Why's that?" his father yelled back through the sweater he was pulling on over his head.

"He was in a really bad mood," Rick said. "He got mad at the Offertory and called me an imbecile!"

"Good grief!" his mother laughed as she turned her face out to the back yard, away from him. He heard his father chuckling down the hall.

It was going to be a good day. He could sense it between them.

"The Good Lord moves in mysterious ways," his mother said.

"He certainly does." His father walked back into the kitchen. He leaned against the stove, looking at Rick directly. "Come on," he said. "Let's move before anyone else gets up and the place goes crazy."

The blue vinyl dashboard was only cracked in two places, and he could hardly see them for they were concealed beneath the ashtray. Except for hundreds of tiny flakes of tobacco — on the seat beneath where his Dad rolled them, and on the glass of the speedometer where he sneezed them out from time to time — the car looked good, almost new. Rick loved to unlatch the steel door of the glove compartment by depressing the nickel-plated button, then listen to it click closed again, firmly, snugly. It was always exciting to be sitting in the car with his father. There was a weight in the motion of the car over the gravel and asphalt that thrilled him. When they were in motion like this it was as if everything was going to be all right. It was another kind of Mass, and depended upon entirely different things that were repeated, but especially the motion: driving into things he couldn't see until he was buried, moving in the midst of them. When his father was behind the wheel like this, when his eyes were concealed behind the aviator sunglasses he wore when he was driving, he was quiet, unshakable, sure of himself. His father had driven a jeep in the war. He'd been a gunner. He was a good driver and Rick loved knowing that.

They passed the bustop on 65th Avenue, heading north on 109th Street. Mr. Bruseker's mother was standing there, wrapped in her gaudy green shawl, ignoring them. Ron Woznow's house flicked by on the right at 68th Avenue. No one was moving around in the yard or the windows. Maybe they're all sleeping, Rick thought. His father put the left signal light on and turned into Jack Knowles' BA station on 70th.

Mr. Knowles came out in his greasy overalls, wiping his hands on the towel he kept tucked in his back pocket, and put a dollar's worth in the car. Rick sat in the car while the two men laughed in the sweet smell that drifted in through the windows. His father was always animated, always laughing and joking when he was talking to people outside the family. His father could be so quiet with him, then be standing there trading jokes with Mr. Knowles. Suddenly, Rick wanted to be older, standing on some gas station asphalt talking about the weather with some guy who worked there, leaning over the trunk of his own car. Out there. It amazed him to think that someday he might have that confidence. So he revelled in his father's gestures: a code he had to crack to get out there himself.

His father leaned back in his seat again, stretching his legs down over the pedals. He rolled a cigarette and lit it before turning the key. He spit the end out onto the floor, and some fine shreds of tobacco stuck to Rick's jeans.

They moved north again. Past Tipton Park where Rick played hockey in the winter. *The Nutty Professor* was still playing at the Varscona Theatre. When they drove through the intersection there he cast his eyes east into all the shops that receded in a blue blur as Whyte Avenue faded into its own never-ending horizon. The shops concealed their secrets in a dark blue haze of mystery and confidence that flickered in the sun so intensely that Rick had to shield his eyes as he squinted into it. Then they were gone. He craned his neck to preserve their image but knew they'd stay the same for him in the end. They wouldn't vanish. They were each of them themselves, he thought. That was it. He was just turning into something. He wasn't really something yet. Everything about himself, he thought, was hesitant, moving into something else. So everything that was itself — the dashboard, the stores in the sun, that couple talking to one another over there at the crosswalk next to the Garneau Theater — amazed him. That they had become something out there. It was wonderful to watch all this, but hard to think about, too. Every now and then he felt he could see what was happening, but the moment would flare and fade, concealing itself again.

Suddenly, the 105th Street Bridge was a steel blue accordion stretched out across the river and if he ignored the flashing black ironwork of the High Level as it clattered by, he could see Renfrew Park lying squat on the north side of the river, and above it, the MacDonald Hotel and the other high buildings that made up Edmonton's skyline in newspaper photos. He imagined an older version of himself suddenly, watching him watch these things. The feeling was so strong he looked behind through the rear window, then sideways at his father's face staring silently ahead. What would he be like when he was as old as his father? Thirty-eight. He peered into the smile lines that creased behind the arm of his father's sunglasses.

He knew life wasn't easy for his father. He was nervous a lot of the time. It was hard to do everything he was supposed to do on his teacher's salary. When Rick tried to see his father from a distance like this, he always wanted to reach over and tell him not to worry about all of them. They were doing all right. He wanted to tell him not to worry, but he couldn't do that. His father would be mad if he said anything. It wasn't his time to say anything. All he could do was become what he was becoming so there might be more confidence in his father's life, so he might laugh with him like Jack Knowles had. That would be something, he thought.

Jasper Avenue. Confusion in every direction. Awnings, sidewalks, alleys, ten-story buildings lurching up and away from the car into the blue. The mystery around him, the certainty of going places, doing things. The CPR Station promised the whole world as it sat so solid, so curled in on itself, so ornate in its bright greens and yellows, hundreds of orange enamel carts clustered near the loading gates, some mysterious design at work.

As they moved north, the giant NADP milk bottle revolved in the sun above its red brick building. Who had thought that up?

His father laughed suddenly, watching him. "It's the rathole for you, my boy!" he said, and the car sped up beneath the tracks on 105th and into the tunnel where all he could see was a small bright circle of air at the far end of it and the random swish of cars that brushed past them in the dark. It was eerie, sitting with his father in this thick dark, moving through it like this. He kept his eyes fastened to the circle of light.

"This is great!" Rick whispered. He was failing his Dad in some way he couldn't see.

They broke out into the sunlight and his father turned right, into McGavin's. He pulled up into the loading area, got out and entered a side door with the sign PERSONNEL ONLY above it.

His father washed trucks down here every second Saturday for loaves of bread. Since he'd started last September, they'd never been short of bread. It was a good deal. That's what his mother kept saying, anyway. Rick rolled his window down and rested his forearm on the glass as his father always did. He could see his father in the half-opened door, a huge bag in his hands, shouting something funny to the people inside. Whatever the punchline to his joke was, it fluttered up to echo in the air above the parking lot, joining all the gulls that hovered and swooped and hesitated up there.

St. Joseph's High School was a cluster of red buildings that sat on a whole city block between 109th and 111th. He had only been here once, a long time ago, when he was four and he and Jane and their mom had brought him his lunch on the bus from the apartment on 124th Street. Now he was going to see where his father worked every day, enter this world they'd heard him talk about in such detail it seemed a mythical landscape they knew by heart. "They installed the drinking fountains in the west wing," he'd tell them at the supper table, "but I don't know how they're going to match the floors."

"Stick with me and don't fool around," his dad said to Rick when he opened the side door to the school with his brass key.

"Okay, Dad," Rick whispered back.

They were walking down a long, gleaming hallway towards a strong square of light. Their shoes echoed off the shiny congoleum and the faint shadows their bodies cast brushed the metal lockers that lined both sides. There were framed photographs above the lockers and two red exit signs shining, but otherwise all he could see with any certainty was his father's body leading him on: the slight slouch of his father's shoulders, the way he bounced as he walked, the sureness of his sense of direction.

He followed his father up a wide flight of stairs that led into another, equally long and dark hallway. They passed two bright drinking fountains trickling water before they turned right down a shorter hallway. Halfway down, on the left-hand side, his father stopped before a large oak door and opened it with one of his keys. The light that sprung out at them seemed unbearable at first because their eyes had grown so accustomed to the thick dark of the hallways, but after he blinked a few times, Rick could see he was standing in his father's classroom.

There were posters on the wall and piles of books on a shelf at the back of the room. In the centre of the blackboard were two columns of three words each: *amo, amas, amat* were in the left hand column, and *amamus, amatis* and *amant* in the right. Rick recognized his dad's handwriting. "What do the words mean, Dad?"

"They're Latin."

"Like in the Mass?"

"That's right," his father said, "just like in the Mass."

"What do those words mean, Dad?"

"That's the conjugation of the verb *to love.*" His father was kneeling down, sorting through a pile of papers on a shelf near the door they'd come through. "It's complicated, but put simply, the words mean *I love, you love, he loves,* and *we love, you love* and *they love.*"

"Oh."

The far side of the room was floor to ceiling windows. Rick looked down on St. Joseph's football field, and, at the far end of that, peeking over the shingled roofs of a row of houses, the white walls of Vic Composite, the protestant High School.

"You just sit down over there. I won't be long."

He sat in one of the desks in the front row and watched his father as he rifled through the oak desk. He watched him take a sheaf of papers over to an upright cupboard and take another from inside that cupboard over to the top of the desk, tie it up with a wide elastic band and place it on the edge of the desk.

Rick imagined his father walking into the room with piles of papers while students shifted in the desks waiting for him to talk. His father's handwriting was everywhere in the room, on white sheets of poster paper pinned to the walls, and on the other blackboards, too. In a couple of places his father had drawn small cartoons next to his writing, to make the students laugh, Rick guessed. He imagined his father walking in here in his suit, away from the fights back home. How could he move through such strange combinations of things that were crazy in one world, and ordered and safe in another? Rick felt a small ache to be in this world with his father, instead of the other one all the time.

His father sat down at the oak desk, heavy and solid beneath the centre of the blackboard, and opened a small notebook.

He made a few entries, then stared at it for a long while, finally looking up at his son, smiling.

"What are you staring at?" he laughed, mocking both of them.

Rick couldn't think of anything to say.

His father looked down at the notebook on the desk again, then sighed. He looked up at Rick.

"Look," he said. "I know you think your old dad's pretty crazy sometimes."

"No Dad, I don't — "

"Just listen to me, Rick," he said. "Listen. Your mother has one way of doing things and I have another. It's always been like that, and there's nothing wrong with either way. They're just different, that's all." His father stretched his arms behind his head and sighed. "Boy oh boy!" he whispered, laughing at himself, then continued. "Anyway, you can't figure everything out all the time. Lots of times it just doesn't figure out, period." He looked up at Rick again, and smiled gently. "I want to show you something I think you should see. Would you like to do that?"

Rick nodded.

"Let's go then." His father got up from the desk and waited for Rick in the doorway.

They were once again in darkness, but the darkness felt thicker now after so much light in the classroom. He followed his father's shape. They retraced their way towards the door they'd come in. Halfway down the second hallway, under a red exit sign, his father stopped at a wide brown door that gave way to a set of stairs descending into the dark. Rick knew they were in the basement; he could hear boilers chugging and radiator pipes hissing behind walls. At the end of another hallway, they reached a door that opened onto another set of stairs, and halfway up these his father stopped at another door. He could hear him fumbling with his key ring, but he couldn't see his face. It was too dark on the stairs. Finally, his father turned a key in the lock and the boy could hear the tumbler click and release. His father pushed the door inward to an even more fathomless dark behind it. This dark had volume. It seemed neverending.

"Go on," his father said.

"But where to?" the boy asked, laughing at his own hesitation for both of them.

"It's all right," his father said, "Just try it."

Rick stopped in the doorway, facing the dark, clenching and unclenching his fists.

"Don't worry, son," his father whispered. "Just see how far you can go. Go on."

The boy gave up and moved into the darkness. There was no choice.

It was a strange sensation. His feet were moving over something smooth and slippery. He could sense enormous space around him in every direction. There seemed no objects near him or in his way. He was walking in inches, guarding himself against whatever his instincts might be protecting him from. He looked back and saw the large, dark shape of his father framed in the doorway. He peered forward again, thinking his eyes might adjust to the dark, but he still couldn't see anything. Just a sense of volume arching over him. He walked faster now, out into the middle of it.

Suddenly, it seemed all right, this dark, and he lost his fear and began to run out into the rest of it. He laughed and shouted back to his father, "I'm running, Dad!" His laughter echoed up into the dark. He was running flat out, abandoning himself to it, when the room exploded with such abrupt light he fell face first on the floor. His hands had shot out automatically and he'd landed softly with his palms out.

He was lying in the middle of the gold, polished floor of the new gymnasium. His father had talked about the building of the gym for months. The floor ran forever in every direction. He took in the bleachers, the basketball hoops, the light fixtures in the ceiling, all the concrete and wires tucked behind them. The room was completely new, completely possible. His father stood in the doorway, his arm extended, his hand on a panel of light switches. Rick glanced around the room again, taking it all in. As he had earlier in the car, he felt an older self staring back down at him from the thickness of the dark. He tried to shake the thought loose for it bothered him, but then gave in to it as he'd given in to the dark moments before. He threw his head back, and as he stared into the endlessness of the height of the place, up into where the ceiling ended, there was something about it he recognized. *Hoc est enim corpus meum.*

He looked back to his father in the doorway. He saw his hand move on the light switch. When the room was claimed by darkness again, Rick could see through it. His father was a small figure now, in a thin square of light, and Rick got up and walked through the dark to join him.

Inversion of Araby's
Labelling + texturizing what has taken place.
Happier endings than Araby.

Roofs

I drove home this weekend to plant annuals with her. I'd been staying in residence in Banff and, though it was unusually hot there for early May, it was also dry. When I turned south into the Okanagan at Sicamous, I rolled the windows down so I could taste the mixture of heat and humidity. All along the twisting highway south, as it hugged the cliffs falling into Mara Lake, I kept thinking, this lush green is going to engulf me.

I'd been cast in an overdone movie about spring, and in this scene the intense greens, in all their variations, were being played off the equally infinite azure blues of these lakes and inland seas.

When I pulled into a service station in Grindrod to get a coffee, I stood for a moment at the back of the place under a weeping willow and watched the Shushwap River threaten its green banks. There was something primeval about the combination of the greens around me and the shuffling weight of the water as it rushed by. Something primeval and simple about my consciousness standing, rooted in itself at the height of this season. I felt a connection, then lost it, and walked back to the car.

As I pulled out onto the highway, the asphalt rushed beneath me, a smooth carpet through the green.

Up the long hill out of Armstrong, just past the Fletcher Challenge Plywood Plant and Roger's Flour Mill, you reach a crest and a bend in the highway. In the middle of this bend, you can see the far hills that cradle Vernon. You know you're almost home when you spot the lofty ridge of Lombardy Poplars on the crest of the hill that separates Vernon from the north end of Okanagan Lake. The Bobslide tourist attraction slips by on the left, then you're in the intersection that feeds Kamloops, and, finally, you're on the last four-lane approach to Vernon. You pass Swan Lake Nurseries on your right, and the long three-mile sweep of Swan Lake itself in the background. On your left, apple orchards curl up the hill in distinct patterns and, here and there, are clusters of homes, no big subdivisions, just homes. Soon a light-industry retail strip surfaces on the left side of the highway: car sales, Bonanza, Arby's, McDonald's. The Village Green Hotel pops up on the left, too, and, simultaneously, the Village Green Shopping Mall on the right. No matter how tacky this strip of retail and tourist traps gets, it is all held by the green. Tall poplars, willows, elms and maples hold the scene and, through the window, on this trip at least, I almost choke on the scent of lilac.

Wherever I look, their pendulous bushes of purple or white sag over picket fences and cracked sidewalks. And the thickness of the greens above and behind the buildings increases as I head south on 27th Street. When I turn left at St. James Catholic Church, and drive south down 26th Street, the sidestreet is canopied with it. She's working in a flower bed at the side of the house, and I notice the Chestnut and the Manitoba Maple have leafed above her. They were just beginning to bud when I left two weeks ago. The Chestnut is over one hundred feet tall and the car I'm driving seems a small thing as I pull into the driveway beneath it.

All weekend we work on the yard. It is endless, for we bought an older home, built in 1917, and it sits on a lot that is eighty feet wide and one hundred and forty feet deep. All the trees and flower beds are on the periphery of the lot, either the outside periphery, or the inside one that hugs the house. In all, there are six flower beds, not including two oak barrels on the patio and three large clay pots on the front porch. The rest of the yard is covered by a lawn that was long and mangy when I pulled in.

We started in on Thursday night and worked through until I left on Sunday. We hauled wheelbarrows of peat and steer manure, drove out to Swan Lake Nurseries to buy more plants, mowed the lawn, and watered all the beds. On Saturday afternoon, in the midst of the 33 C heat, I was hosing down the sidewalks after mowing the lawn. I could smell the water on the cement next to the cut grass and something kept pushing my memory. I realized it was this precise combination — hand, hose, cold water, cement sidewalk and cut grass — that was completely familiar. My memory works that way. It opens like a flower at the precision of smell. When it happens, before I get a chance to think about it, there is a passage backwards that's physical. The memory presents itself as a concrete thing. I am in another landscape.

Sometimes we use metaphors because they carry us — like the hand, hose, water, cement and grass — farther into what happened rather than away from it. I don't know. I struggle with this all the time.

I'm ten years old. I'm lying flat on the lawn in our backyard in Edmonton. It's spring and I've been helping my dad dig the potato patch, but I'm taking a break now. He's still digging over there in the far corner of the patch, beneath the poplars. He mowed the lawn early this morning before we got up, and my mother just hosed down the patio, then disappeared into the house to make egg salad sandwiches. We're going to have them out here, apparently, and that's why she hosed down the patio. Susan and Mary-Lou are helping her in the kitchen. I can hear Harry playing road hockey with Greg and Wayne in the alley. Frankie's looking after Michael in the sandbox. Michael's only one and has a little white cotton bonnet on. Frankie's helping him build roads in the sandbox. Michael just keeps looking at him, drooling. The roads are for Frankie. I can see and hear all this from my spot. I close my eyes.

I feel my cheek on the grass. Several blades stick into my mouth, and my tongue is playing with them, noticing their sharpness, tasting the green. I smell the wet cement and the grass together, and wonder what wheel holds us together like this? Who invented it? Is it true we're going camping in Banff in early July? Is this a firm plan, or will they fight it out and maybe change it? We have such a good time when we're camping. Dad doesn't drink, and Mom gets lost in all the details of what to bring, what to eat, where we'll go. She loves writing away for brochures and planning everything out. That's what she's like. My dad is the opposite. He always gives her a hard time about being so organized.

My dad was in the war. He grew up in Westville, Nova Scotia, a small coal town a few miles from New Glasgow, just in from the coast. His father was the principal of the high school there, and after the war my dad went to St. FX, then Columbia University in New York, so he could teach too. He met my mother at a dance in Moncton just before the war, and they corresponded while he was overseas. In 1946, they got married and lived in Antigonish while my dad went to university. They had three of us there — Susan, me and Harry — and during the last two years in Antigonish, my dad was away a lot, completing his degree in New York, while we stayed home. Finally, in 1952, he got a job out west, in Edmonton. The

Separate School Board was desperately looking for teachers, and the salary they offered — $4500.00 — doubled what he made working as Registrar at St. FX. In the summer of 1952, he moved out to Edmonton ahead of us and rented a two-bedroom apartment on 124th Street.

We came by train in early September, stopping off to visit our relatives all over the maritimes before we left. After the cramped days in tiny compartments on the train, my mother ushered us into the vast, arching vault of the Southside Station. It was full of people moving beneath the still, catapulting beams arching way over our heads in an intricate pattern of joists and steel rivetting. They seemed quiet compared to the jostling bodies and voices chattering beneath them. And, suddenly, there he was in his grey sportscoat, a hat pulled down over his forehead on an angle, a cigarette dangling from his lips. His familiar half smile loomed over us as he gave our mother a kiss, almost shy.

Within a year, my parents bought a house on 61st Avenue, north of the Cemetery Hill, just west of the Calgary Trail. Thousands of people like us had moved out to the city after the war and that, plus the developments in the oil business, meant that many new suburbs like ours were being built. Between 1952 and 1961, my parents had four more children: Frankie, Mary-Lou, Michael and Timmy. They developed the basement eventually so we could live in the house and not fall over one another all the time.

I guess we were lucky our parents moved us out west in the early fifties even though it meant being cut off from our relatives. We were set down in the land of opportunity at exactly the right time. It was open in the west then and everything was possible. Our minds were forged in a new world, I think, and we carried it in us, like a seed. The blossoming of that seed has always mystified me: to have grown a mind that lives in the world and stares into it with hybrid eyes, striving for a communion with the physical that seems an impossible thing to want in the face of everything else sometimes, but the only antidote for a restlessness that comes with that sight. It fascinates me, and every time I try to write, it's as if I am writing out of this thick, impossible world I grew up in, and out of all the voices chattering in it. I cannot break free of it and, I guess, in the long run I don't want to. I don't know. It's hard to say.

I'm always crawling under it, seeking shelter.

She has just rounded the corner of the house with a flat of begonias. I turn off the hose, and join her at the three pots on the front steps. I dig the holes, she plants the begonias. We don't talk, but we're smiling in the shade: to live this simply, to delight in something as simple as this after all that has happened.

Sunday at noon, I'm heading back to Banff to write this down. We embrace in the driveway. I'll be back to do the same thing next weekend. We already know what we'll be planting then. She'll pick up the rest of the annuals during the week.

When I pull onto the highway the car is smooth in the heat, the windows down again. The bright fields fold by in waves, and my coffee cup empties itself slowly as the miles roll by. I am already reaching for metaphors that will catch all this so it won't wheel as uncontrollably as those crows flickering in the afternoon sky near Revelstoke.

A family of five lives in a stucco house in south Edmonton. The parents, Charles and Colette, are from the maritimes and have moved their three children — Jane, Rick and Neil — out west, away from the past.

Everything is happening at once.

When I reach for a cigarette and light it, their voices compete with one another. They're trying to tell me something.

They won't let up.

Room

It sometimes happened that I'd look at my table and repeat: 'It's a table, it's a table,' until a shy thrill appeared that I'd christen joy.

— Jean-Paul Sartre, *The War Diaries*,
(written in The Alsace near Strasbourg)
November 1939 - March 1940.

The war that had ended fifteen years before still weighed on my mind, and I felt that before many years there would be another.

— Elias Canetti, "Strasbourg 1933",
The Play Of The Eyes.

He still got a kick out of the car. Even after driving it nine months, Rick couldn't believe they'd bought it. Since they'd started living together, he and Jennifer had always driven wrecks he'd picked up for nothing. They couldn't afford anything else. They'd driven them until they collapsed, then snivelled and crawled to various loan officers to get another one.

He'd logged thousands of miles criss-crossing the country faking sureness for her, knowing the radiator could blow, the valves seize, the muffler drop off. And even though he'd gotten used to it, he'd logged those miles tense: looking in the rear-view mirror for cops, watching the heat gauge wondering if they'd make the next town, worrying about a faulty tire she didn't know about.

Each of those old cars was as vivid to him now, as he signalled to pull out and pass a Winnebago south of Sicamous, as the rooms he and Jennifer had lived in over those years. Each one had a quality, a set of details he could summon up as clearly as the curtains they'd put up in Toronto, rug remnants they'd laid down in a living room in Regina, the Norfolk Pine they'd installed in their bedroom in Vernon when they'd first moved to the Okanagan.

Now, after ten years, they'd bought a house, too. A house and a car he could count on. A new car. What's happening to my life, he wondered. Where is this safety coming from?

He slowed down behind a half-ton doing eighty. The other side of the highway was too thick with traffic to pass. He'd wait. It was all right. The four lane stretch at Malaqua was coming up in five kilometers.

A five year old boy in a Vernon Lakers baseball cap stared out the back window of the half-ton at him, smiling. Rick waved. The kid waved back, made a goofy face, then turned away.

He drummed his fingertips on the steering wheel and inhaled the car. A nineteen-ninety Toyota Tercel. Only driven by him. It was his car. He grinned around at the interior, laughing at himself. He felt like a kid again. It always surprised him when he caught himself excited like this, when he discovered he could still get thrilled, still have that innocence. He loved seeing it in other people. He loved creating it for them. It was his strength to do that for other people. For Jennifer. He never expected it for himself.

He was too guarded for it.

So he laughed as he pulled out to pass the half-ton in Malaqua. The sleek black shape of the Tercel made him feel he was in a sports car, and its grace and weight defined him suddenly. He laughed at this moment of innocence. It was too small and too big at the same time. The Tim Horton's coffee cup rested perfectly in the plastic pull-out tray above the ashtray. Everything worked in here. Everything was new. He fumbled on the passenger seat for his cigarettes, pushed in the lighter to the right of the ashtray, and lit a smoke. As he returned the lighter to its sleeve, he felt its steel and plastic slide smoothly into place and lock with a perfect click. Everything had its place, its function. He didn't have to pretend, even to himself.

I love creating it for other people. Why did I just think that? Why did it come to me in that particular way?

Because I'm good at joy, he admitted. I'm good at creating it around me. Not for myself, but for others. It's a gift and a curse, and I learned it young and well. Rick understood its function in his life now, and he'd learned the hard way to get past it, to make a bit of joy for himself, finally. But like the car and the house, this safety made him uneasy.

His new running shoes gleamed up at him from the floor as if they had a life of their own.

"If you're going to go up there," Jennifer had laughed, "you might just as well go in style."

He'd been sitting in the store at the mall, unopened boxes of running shoes spread in a pile around his feet. He could sense the earnest salesman hovering as he'd caught Jennifer's eyes.

"They fit really well," he'd confessed, staring at how awkward they looked on his feet, almost obscene against his old jeans.

"Well, it's simple," she'd sighed, looking at him and then at the salesman. "He'll take them."

Afterwards, she'd hauled him into The Bay to try on jeans and sweaters until, finally, after an hour of struggling, she had him outfitted for the trip.

He hated doing this, and she knew it. He despised the glimpses of himself in the three way mirrors in those small change rooms. The only reason he'd put up with it was because he felt guilty about going on this trip without her. He knew how pleased she'd be to dress him up for it. By the time they'd gotten home, she was triumphant. She made him model everything for her again, and though it was the last thing he wanted to do, he did it.

"You look great," she'd said, finally, shaking her head. "I just can't understand why you don't ever do this for yourself. On your own."

He'd laughed and shook his head. "I know, I know. My whole family's like this. It's not my fault entirely."

He had to slow down for a one-lane bridge under construction two kilometers west of Beardale Castle. A semi had pulled off the side of the road and he could see its driver squatting down at the back, checking a tire. As he passed the last orange arch of the bridge, as it swept into the rear view mirror, he could smell the strong scent of cedar through the open window and see three crows devouring a porcupine.

He'd crept into their room early, just after seven. The car was packed. He'd put his suitcase, stuffed with new clothes and notebooks, into the trunk after he'd showered. Everything fit so neatly into the trunk. He'd stood there in the carport for a moment, staring into the trunk's perfection, even its soft click of closure.

He hadn't been able to sleep. He'd sat out on the couch until three, reading Elias Canetti's *The Play Of The Eyes.* When he'd finished, he'd browsed through Sartre's Alsatian war diaries, written when Sartre had begun to understand subjectivity. He'd been drawn to both writers for different reasons, but more recently, he'd been intrigued by a coincidence that linked him to them. Both Sartre and Canetti had spent time in Strasbourg, France, at crucial junctures in their lives, and so had he. He and Jennifer had lived in Strasbourg for a year in 1988, and for him it had been the turning year. He'd seen something in those streets, about himself and his world, that had opened a door for him. He'd stood on the roof of that ancient Cathedral and stared out at the roofs of Strasbourg interlacing their chipped chalk field below him; he'd stared beyond them into the green forests and orchards that lipped the dark blue Vosges, and he'd understood something about the rooms he'd shaped for himself in his life, and the rooms his culture had shaped for him as well. He'd stood in the vortex of his history and understood something, and ever since he'd been looking for others who'd seen it, too. Later, when he discovered both Sartre and Canetti had stood there, it seemed a crazy gift and he puzzled over it like this often, sitting up late on couches, breathing over thumbed and marked pages in the dawn.

Before he slept, he'd written in his own notebook. He'd written about how he was feeling, what he'd like to accomplish on the trip aside from visiting his family. In the end, he'd made a list of the things he'd do, the articles he'd collect in the library, the people he'd call while he was in Edmonton.

He'd always made these lists, then never looked at them again. The act of making them seemed to secure a clear room for him in advance: a passage into something circumscribed. Making the lists protected him, eased his fear of inertia, of being alone and unattended. It was an obvious psychological game, and though he saw through it, he still needed to play it. Finally, after he'd slept on the couch for a couple of hours, he'd gotten up at six, showered, packed the car, and stood in their bedroom, leaning over Jennifer as she slept. Her hands were folded almost in prayer. He kissed her on the cheek.

"I'm leaving," he whispered.

She groaned, plowed her face farther into the pillow, then blinked up at him. "OK. You have a wonderful time."

"Don't worry," he whispered, "I will."

"Say hi to everyone up there for me," she sighed and flicked her head back into the pillow.

"Don't worry. I will."

He stood and watched her as she drifted back into sleep. He did feel guilty about going on the trip without her.

He knew why.

In the old days when he'd done this, he'd always returned sheepish, exhausted, his sunglasses concealing the damage. She'd always known in advance what would happen. He'd set off with great intentions, his lists clearly marked in his notebooks. He would have a good, healthy time by himself. He'd visit his family and friends and have good visits. But each time, his heart had accelerated with the car as he'd pulled away from the rooms they lived in, and he'd known in his gut that what he was going to do when he got there was lose himself for days with whoever could keep up with him. Lose himself as completely as he could. Each time, when it was over, he'd be sitting in the car driving back wondering who had gone on the trip. As he'd shifted his body behind the steering wheel those times, there was always the eerie sensation he was two people, that somewhere beneath his affection and earnestness — the person he seemed to be most of the time — was a self that wanted other things, wanted to undermine the life he'd built so carefully with Jennifer, the life he cherished. It was the strangest feeling. He was never ready for it.

He'd looked around the bedroom before he left, feeling its detail with his eye: the soft, web-like fronds of the Norfolk Pine under the white enamel wood of the windowledge, the pale yellow cotton of the curtains through which the spring air was shifting, the gleam of the brass rail that connected one side of the amber pine bedrail to the other, her body curled into itself beneath the mauve quilt.

The electric clock clicked beside the bed. Her hand twitched occasionally in the dark, the index finger pointing at the face of the clock like the finger of God on the Sistine Chapel ceiling. He'd looked around the room, inhaling it, memorizing it, tucking it away in the corner of his head where his lists waited, where he hoped to live forever.

He pulled into a truckstop just west of the Enchanted Forest. The place was empty except for an older man sitting in the far corner by himself, reading the *Calgary Herald*. The highway insisted itself through the windows of the place and he was always aware of its constant motion as he stood over the open glass countertop, his keys dangling from one hand, the other hand flat on the smooth, cool glass above the rows of Chiclets, Trident gum and Lifesavers.

The waitress behind the till couldn't have been more than eighteen. She was cute. Her hair had been permed and it bounced around the dimples on her cheeks as she squinted at him and grinned. She had that mischievous quality some young women possessed, a curiosity in her eyes that was older than her body. He ordered two take-out coffees. He figured he could drive straight through Revelstoke and the Rogers Pass to Golden if he got two coffees and drank them slowly. She disappeared into the kitchen and returned with the styrofoam cups. She snicked the lids down after she'd put in the cream and sugar. She took his bill and gave him the change. "Going to Vancouver?" she smiled at him.

"No," he said, "I'm heading to Edmonton to visit my folks."

"That's nice," she replied, and gave him a final smile.

As he juggled the cups through the glass door, he laughed out loud at himself. Why did I tell her I was visiting my folks? She wouldn't care. She'd only asked him to pass the time.

Before he pulled the seatbelt around himself, he bit the plastic lids in two places then secured them again so he wouldn't have any spills. He passed his hand over the pebbly black finish of the dashboard, then reached for the steel end of the seatbelt and drove it home until it clicked, secure, tight. The car drifted forward silently, humming over the crushed gravel, gaining the smooth asphalt that would draw him over the pass to Golden. He sighed to himself, pleased. Everything was in order. Everything was working. He felt elated, almost in tears, and he didn't know why.

He did know why.

He pulled into a rest stop east of the summit. He needed to get rid of the coffee, and when he finished he sat for a moment at one of the picnic tables that circled a small, pine kiosk. The kiosk displayed historical information and hiking maps under glass for tourists. He lit up a smoke and looked down into the long, pendulous valley that stretched away beneath him and curled south to Golden. This was a big room. As he looked out onto the pine forests and the sharp edges of mountains that fell away into themselves for what seemed forever, he felt the tears again, unsummoned. He relaxed.

He had no room he was protecting within himself anymore. He had been delivered into the real world again, all of it, any of it. He could sit on this pine bench, and look out into these mountains and feel he belonged. He had nothing to hide anymore, no reason to turn away. He was part of it or could be part of it. It was hard to get used to, this feeling, especially when he realized how long he'd avoided it, how hard he'd resisted.

The wind brushed his beard, his cheeks, his hair.

He'd left the room that had concealed him from everything, that had grown so small in the end. The reward was that he'd been ushered into a much larger one, into everything itself. He'd become every detail in the air.

He'd seen this in other people, protected it in them when he'd had the chance to, but he never expected it for himself. In some ways, he'd done everything to make sure he'd be denied it.

He'd seen it in other people.

When he'd gone straight, and he'd stared into all the paradoxes that had held him shimmering there in his own self-inflicted light, he'd been delivered out of one version of himself into another that was waiting: shy, embarrassed, and hopeful. He'd never felt so vulnerable in his life, and he'd never felt so mad. He'd never resisted anything so fiercely as that delivery. It had taken a long time. Finally, he'd given up the self that measured everything, controlled each detail. He'd given up and, surprise! No one had been more surprised than him, more humbled. It was all new, all difficult, and he still felt that way four years later, sitting at this picnic table, inhaling the mountain air; in, then out, in, then out. Long draughts, big swallows of it. Surprise! What he'd recovered was his life, the world, time.

It was bigger than him. It was Strasbourg. That's when he'd first felt it deeply. He'd stayed up one night, staring out their apartment window into all these things then, too. It had been another room, like this one, here. And even as it had opened, as his heart had raced to meet the clarity among the pigeons and the roofs and the sun, he'd warned himself he couldn't keep it all in his head, he'd have to let it go. But he'd stood there anyway, looking out into everything until he understood he was everything he was looking at. Jennifer had been asleep behind him in the living room. He was just standing there, leaning against the windowframe, smoking. Booze had always delivered the promise of texture. It was one thing about it that fascinated him, a sudden focus on detail that was a kind of relief. But it had carried him away from things in the end. It had made the world smaller, and set up a barrier between him and things. The barrier was protection from the terror of the clarity he'd experienced that night in Strasbourg. It wasn't easy to stand in that light, see so much that was wonderful and awful. It wasn't easy to grow up and become everything. There was no protection now, but nothing like the clarity, either. He'd never had a bigger buzz, and he'd never had to work so hard to get it. In the end a huge, fracturing Alsatian Easter sun had broken through the eaves and the sounds the sparrows made, and had lifted him beyond irony for the rest of his life.

He turned into Smitty's, on the long strip of gas stations and motels in Golden. Beside it stood the Golden Rest Motel where he and Jennifer had stayed once years ago, heading back to Vernon from Regina. They hadn't been able to stand the thought of four more hours in the shaky old Aspen they'd been driving.

That had been fun. He could recall the hardboard of the walls in the room, the ridiculous painting of a waterfall that hung over the TV, their disappointment when they could only get one channel and had to watch *The Beachcombers* and *Front*

Page Challenge while three flies flailed around inside the plastic light fixture on the ceiling.

He can't believe he's standing here in the motel office, paying for a room. It's crazy, but he accepts the key and walks back out into the parking lot. He positions the car in front of 8A, opens the trunk, and hauls the suitcase into the room. What am I doing, he wonders, but ignores the question easily. He takes out his notebook and places it in the center of the desk to the right of the TV. He opens the drapes so the late morning sun snickers into the room. He stares past the asphalt and the powerlines, past the constantly shifting colours of the cars and trucks whipping by on the highway, out into the mountain that rips upwards into the sky. There's a fierceness about it.

He looks back at the notebook lying in the center of the desk. He has set his pen in the middle of an open page, a blank page.

The drive down into Golden is easy and he finds the liquor store quickly. He buys a twenty-six of Canadian Club. He watches himself do this. His fingers are trembling when he pays for it, and his eyes furtive, glancing over his shoulder, waiting for a disaster, a voice to announce, "You can't do this. I'm sorry. You'll have to come with me."

Back in the room, he draws the curtains closed, switches on the table lamp by the side of the bed, sets the unopened bottle of rye on the desk beside his notebook, and stares into this world. What is happening to me, he wonders. Another voice tells him to relax, lighten up. We're just going to take it easy for a bit. You deserve this. You've done so well. It's a small thing. You've always been too serious.

He sits down at the desk and grabs his pen. At the top of the blank page, he writes, "What am I doing to myself? It will be all right."

He sets the pen down and takes the bottle and twists off its cap. The paper that seals the cap cracks in the air. He leans back in the chair and takes a long swallow. He shakes his head as it runs down into his stomach. His hands are shaking. He can feel the beginnings of the rye in his blood. It feels good. He has crossed over.

It feels like fire, a room of its own. He's back. This is familiar, this place, and he laughs as he closes his eyes. He's sweating now. He can feel the small drops bead on his forehead and the tip of his nose.

Fucking relief, that's all. Another kind of joy. Who's to say? Running around, trying to be a decent person, holding everything in. Who gives a shit sometimes, really? You can't run around like that, holding everything tight to your chest, measuring out everything in your fucking day? It can't work like that. You need room. What about all this energy here? What about the self that doesn't want all those lines and grids? What's wrong with not wanting all that crap? There's nothing wrong except noboby loves you when you don't want that. When you want this. Everybody gets scared. Too bad.

The only thing that's real is this head and what it does, the white terror of it. Everything else we invent to comfort ourselves, but it isn't real. It's all just stage machinery, some nice play about a life that has order, all shadow boxing.

What about all this energy, now? Where does it go? How can I exorcise it? By denying it, pretending I don't have it? Trying to be somebody else, somebody different from me, somebody who knows how to be happy in a simple, normal way? I don't know anything.

I like doing this. It feels good. It feels like home. I only don't do it when I get afraid. Afraid of losing Jennifer, afraid of losing the life I've made without it, that little house with the tree in the bedroom. Life's too short to be afraid all the time and I wish I didn't fall into that fear as easily as I do. I should just be this, here, and fuck what anybody thinks. It won't matter in the long run, that's for sure.

It's funny when you think about it. There's these two funerals, see? In the first a small group of sedately dressed people stand and watch as a coffin is lowered. Finally, one of them, a woman dressed rather primly, whispers, "He was a decent human being!" Just down from this funeral, another coffin is being lowered. There are loads of people swaying above this one. They're all laughing and crying as the coffin disappears. "What a wretched, spoiled, selfish wonderful prick he was!" some woman yells out, "No! Let's be honest! A real rat's ass if there ever was one." She catches a deep gutteral sob in her throat and holds one hand out over the casket in an improvised blessing. "He'd have loved that metaphor," she continued, "the stupid, glorious angel he was!" Everyone else laughs and shakes his or her head in the rain, crying for how crazy this person was, how wild, how restless, how loved. The first group drives off to sit in a dark living room somewhere; the second bunch goes to the bar. Hah!

My family is waiting somewhere, aren't they? Laughing? I don't know.

Those poplars in the back yard, swaying in the summer above us in the early morning, and Neil and I'd be there, wrapped up in our sleeping bags on the lawn. We'd sleep out there every night in the summer. It hardly ever rained on us. And sometimes Dad'd sit up late with us. He'd be drinking, relaxing, chatting away as the dark descended and took our neighbourhood away into the sky somewhere. And sometimes Jane'd be sitting there in a lawnchair in the morning with a cup of tea, waiting for us, and the lawn would smell that deep green summer smell and the poplars would flick and sway and switch their branches gently over the fence, click, shuffle, pop in the dark and in the morning light.

And they're all sitting somewhere now, too, aren't they? We're not lying under those poplars anymore, we're out leading these lives separated by highways and mountains and time and things we have to do in the sun to get by, to create lives with other people.

Ah, the thickness of things that speak in the dark and of things that don't speak, don't have the language to say what they are.

I love the way my hand stretches out, the veins in it moving my blood, the sigh of my brain as it settles down into itself here in the dark of this sunny day. I hear noises around me somewhere, but they're faint, vague noises, and it's as if there is no detail finally, only this fire right here, in my eye.

There are no walls. I can walk through everything with this smile, this magical smile I only get this way. I can see through everything and there are no boundaries, nothing to enclose anything, and each object evanesces into air, there are no details no edges to anything, and this is the way it should be in the sun, under the moon.

I can see myself sitting with my dad in a car and we're driving somewhere, through things somewhere and we don't care whether it's dark or light where we're going, and there's Neil suddenly, too, he's sitting in a car with Shelley and they're driving, too, into mountains on a highway somewhere, and here's Jane now, walking down a path through some trees I don't recognize, looking for something. I can see the smile lines around her eyes squinting into the sun. And my mom and dad are sitting in an apartment, flicking through channels on the TV, and my mom has just announced she's going to bed, and Dad just said he'd sleep in the guest room because of her cold, and everything is drawing everything else into itself, and we're all whirling in a room with no detail and no walls somewhere.

As if while my world contracts, it expands in my head so I can see it.

To lose everything like this so you can get it all back somehow. Ah! You need room for that.

He reached over and picked up the coffee he'd bought in Smitty's. His hands were shaking. He sighed. After all this time. A room that could only get smaller until it destroyed him. He'd hesitated, his coffee waiting for him, even the car a small room he was barrelling over the planet in.

In the car he'd rested his forehead on the steering wheel. He was sweating. All he could do was close his eyes, take the key, slip it into the ignition and watch as the car moved out over the gravel and onto the highway.

As he rose on the winding road that carried him above Golden and into the pass, the spruce and pine closed in on either side while ravens and hawks flickered in the distances. He was driving into himself, into the possible: the delicate hum of the tires on the asphalt, the plummeting steel weight of the car careening forward into the blue air.

He pulled into the gas station in Field. He phoned Jennifer from a pay phone and told her to put out the water for the dog. He'd forgotten all about the water for the dog. It hadn't been on his list.

He walked over to the car, opened the trunk, pulled the notebook out of the suitcase and tossed it into the heavy blue Laidlaw dumpster that squatted like a tarnished grail in the dust behind the service station.

Re introduces dog + lists in order to stabalize himself.

Roofs in the Rain

You go back to another time. Not everyday. Not like that. Not often, even. I don't know. I'm sitting here tonight on the couch, too tired to sleep. *The Bay Boy* is on the TV with the sound down. Images of Nova Scotia in the '30s. 1937, in fact. Glace Bay. My father's time in Westville. He'd have been fifteen. Running over the coal-dust street toward the corner store with the red sign. The green roof. Rain like gauze between the corners of the wet, enamel buildings and the deep, flat green of the trees behind them, closing in on them. A mist whites the cinder town. You go back to another time. No one invites you. It just happens.

You go back to another time. You try to sometimes. It's a retreat, I suppose. When you want protection from something here. Or you want to retrieve something, discover something you never knew, maybe. Whatever it is, you need it now, here. You go back to another time to get it.

You go back to another time. Whatever it is you need there is not a lie, though it isn't something anyone who was there would have known or seen or smelled either. Not that, even. Like your dad in those black shoes in the rain. He never knew, maybe, what it is you've gone back for. It doesn't matter. Whatever is back there is in your head and that's why you have to go. That's what's there. And whatever it is, it's what you need. So you go back there to get it. That's what's true.

I sat on the porch steps tonight in the dark. Three times. I was sitting out there having a smoke. That's what I do now. I don't smoke in here. I sit out there. And as I was sitting out there Orion shifted from left to right in the night sky in four hours. It seemed strange. That it was so obvious. A young boy ran by heading east up the hill the third time I sat there. I heard his boots click, muffled against the snow as he ran. I could spot him occasionally in the streetlight's wake. Then I looked up to see The Hunter and his belt. His sword. Orion hanging above the shining red roof of the house across from us. It's shining because it's metal, and it's metal because of the snow. The snow won't stay on it as it stays on our grey asphalt roof. I like to see that bright red shining roof under the stars alongside the streetlights. There is something about it that's vibrant, comforting. Especially when it's raining. When it's raining or snowing I can still sit there and smoke because the overhang above our porch protects me. I don't get wet. Maybe my shoes do a bit. Maybe I have to edge the ashtray in a bit, too. But, basically, it's all right in the rain. Though I don't see the stars then. I don't see Orion on those nights.

Think of the People Behind You

"You never told me you thought that!"

"I'm telling you now."

"Well, why haven't you ever said that before?"

"I don't know. It just didn't come up. That's all."

"Didn't come up!"

"Well, it didn't somehow. Really!"

"I don't know about you, Neil."

"I'm sorry."

"Didn't come up!"

"Really."

"Well, do you believe what you just said?"

"—"

"*Do you?*"

"I don't know, Shelley."

"You *must* know."

"I don't."

"God, you piss me off sometimes!"

"I'm sorry."

"No kidding!"

They'd been on the road three hours and had seven to go. They'd just taken the Cochrane bypass of Calgary by slipping off Highway Two at Carstairs. It was a scenic bypass if you had the time, if you were feeling up for it and had innocent eyes.

They'd driven straight through on Thursday. The funeral had been on Friday. They'd stayed with his mother two more days and were now whisking back, exhausted, at the end of things. It was Monday. They both had to work tomorrow. They were thinking about everything.

They both remembered other trips, at least one a year for the last six years. On most of those trips they'd felt carefree; they'd laughed a lot.

They'd been together for fifteen years. There was nothing each of them didn't know about the other person squinting into the sun through the windshield beside them. Nothing. That's what both of them had come to believe. They both believed, too, that it was this kind of confidence, this sure knowledge they each had of the other, that had kept them together while so many couples they knew had separated. The knowledge had steadied them to one another through everything else that had happened.

It was the middle of a May afternoon, and through the mild heat haze, they could see the mountains in the distance over Carstairs. It was Neil's favourite time to drive. He loved spring on the prairies.

Ever since he'd been a little boy, and his father had taken him and his brother and sister on a trip through Banff and Jasper, he'd fallen in love with the smell, the intricate excitement of it: slipping across the asphalt while the smells of hay and mustard seed and clover filtered through the half-opened windows; closing the car door over the crushed gravel of a service station parking lot, smelling the air, seeing the wideness of things, the way things never ended out on the prairies; going in and getting a coke, glancing sideways to see his dad checking the oil in the station wagon, seeing him lean over the hood, peer intently into the engine while around him in the sky flicked spring sparrows who had chosen the gas station as their home. There had been moments back then, with his dad and his brother and sister, when his own excitement in things was matched by the things themselves. There had been those wonderful crossings when what was going on inside his head seemed also to be going on outside, in the air that cradled him, in the soft summer grasses he could see through the car window as he imitated his dad by resting his elbow and forearm on the cool glass and felt. There had been those times back then.

He'd just said to her, casually, thinking of his dad, that he didn't think it was possible to know anyone else, that inner lives were too complex to be seen by another person. She'd stared at him in the silence. On another day, on another trip, she might have thought about the statement and talked it over with him. It might have been innocent enough: a theory to be picked over, an idea to swivel around in the air between them. But today she was exhausted and frightened, though she didn't know why she was frightened. She just was.

She looked over at his eyes squinting through his cheap sunglasses. She breathed him in, every detail: his small nose that wriggled under the sunglasses to keep them afloat, the smile lines that crinkled beneath his eyes, his peppered beard that looked so trimmed because he'd spruced himself up for the funeral. She knew how vulnerable he was feeling behind those glasses. She knew how close he'd been to his dad, how shocked he'd been when his brother had woken him with the news. She knew him so well she could understand how he could slip now, for weeks, into a soft depression in which he would mull everything over arduously, turn everything about himself outward to be examined under a caustic light only he could turn on himself. She knew this was going to happen. She knew, too, because she'd watched him for so long, that there was an innocence, a core in him that loved everything, and, as always, this core would take over in the long run and save him from himself, save him for her. Then he would focus on her again; he would rise up out of his privacy and love her again. It was all very predictable. She was used to it. What frightened her this time was what he'd said. He'd never said that before. It didn't sound like him to be saying it. It ran against his instincts. Maybe this time will be different, she wondered, maybe this time he won't surface with his smile in the end, won't turn to me finally with that old, innocent grin.

So she pushed him. She wanted to know what he meant so she could counteract it. She wasn't going to give in, allow him to slip away from her for too long. She knew this man. She loved him.

He hated fighting with her; it made him panic. They'd always had to make up, both of them. Neither of them could let a fight go. It had to be solved before either of them could rest. Sure, they both made compromises sometimes so a fight could be solved, but, basically, they knew enough to solve them. In the long run, each time, they'd return to the common ground they both believed nourished them. He could sense her sulking over by the window, withdrawing, plotting something to throw him off, make him be honest instead of oblique. But there was a rift between them now and he knew he *was* the rift. He felt they'd been playing games with one another all along. It had all been a ruse, this togetherness, this false knowledge.

He squinted over at her and wondered who this person was, how he'd ended up at forty sitting in a car with her. She wasn't his family. She didn't know what they knew about him. She wasn't his dad joking away at him, making fun of him, knowing everything about him there was to know. He felt a great loneliness about who and where he was. He felt a longing to be a child again, to sit next to his dad in the dark of the car as his dad's fingers thrummed the steering wheel, as his dad's voice made soft announcements about how far they were, when they'd arrive. It startled him to be flooded with this longing for him and this fear of her. He understood these feelings were predictable. He'd just been to his father's funeral. It was natural. He got mad at his brain that would play this kind of trick on him, conspire to remove the very person he needed to comfort him and replace her with an emptiness he felt he was falling through, away from this world here, away from the hay in those fields, the tires whispering over the asphalt. Where was he being taken? How separate was the place he seemed to be going to? Why had he said what he'd said?

When I stared down at him lying in that open coffin, he thought, I saw an image of separateness. It wasn't just the fact of death that had summoned the image. It wasn't that obvious. He'd looked down into the coffin to make peace with himself, too. He'd stared down into his own love for his father and found it separate, mysterious, over. It was hard to even think about. There were no words to make a ritual out of what he'd seen, turn the crossing into something clear, something formalized, something complete and full of love. Love, he sighed. He'd whispered their old saying into his father's ear and kissed him on the forehead. Then he'd faltered down the aisle and out into this confusion. He adjusted the visor to protect his eyes. He wanted the world back. He wanted his love for it back. There were no words to explain to her how he felt. He would have to pretend.

"But we do know each other," she whispered, her face turned away out the passenger window, "we do share that."

"I know," he said. "Don't pay any attention to me, Shelley. I'm tired and confused. That's all. I don't know what I'm talking about. Forget it."

She looked over and reached across and placed her hand on his. It was resting on the gear shift. The tiny hairs above his freckles felt like strands of silk. She could feel them moving. She could feel the touch of his skin like a landscape. This was the man she thought she loved. She didn't believe what he'd just said about ignoring him. He was pretending.

When they wheeled into Cremona a small cluster of buildings popped up from the trees suddenly like a cartoon as they made a sharp turn around the last corner. There was a small café they both liked there.

"Do you feel like a coffee, a treat?" he asked her.

"Sure."

He drove onto the gravel in front of the café. As he eased himself out of the car he could hear whippoorwills chattering like a feast in the blue air. The sun shed a harsh gold over everything, and made each detail crisp, sharp, focused. Why don't I feel like I usually feel, he muttered to himself, then tucked the sadness away and grinned for her as they walked into the café.

The café was packed with farmers and truckers. Eight of them had pulled two tables together by the window. Neil and Shelley slipped into the à la carte line that bordered the long, stainless steel trays of sandwiches, salad plates, juices, desserts, and fruit. At the end of this line were two stainless steel coffee urns; one held coffee, the other water for tea. He remembered them from the last time and smiled for the strange convolutions of his brain, the weird things it would exult over.

The table of eight men lined up behind them. Shelley was fussing over the sandwiches. She didn't know if she wanted egg salad, which looked pretty good she thought, or chicken salad, which looked even better.

"The only problem is you can never tell about the chicken ones," she whispered to him. "Sometimes they're OK. Sometimes they're not."

He looked up and noticed the cashier peering down the aisle, waiting for them. He could imagine feet shifting vaguely in one spot behind him. Shelley was pretty standing there in her bright city clothes. She looked completely out of place in this small café. She appeared sophisticated, he thought, and was almost embarrassed by her, by what the men behind him might be thinking about her. Neither of them belonged here. For some reason, he felt sad about that. He also felt a nervousness overtake him.

Shelley always took a long time to select anything. She worried she'd get the wrong thing. She got frustrated in restaurants with him, too, for the opposite reason. He knew what he wanted. He always ordered something Irish, something that stuffed. "It was growing up in my family that did it," he'd said to her. "You never want to run out. You always want to have some backup, or something that'll do the trick completely." She'd look at him anxiously as he tucked into a clubhouse sandwich with fries, worrying that her subtle crab salad wasn't going to leave her satisfied in the end, wasn't going to deliver as his most certainly was. This was an old joke between them, but today, standing in the lineup with these people behind them waiting, he felt annoyed with her, embarrassed. "Come on," he thought to himself, "Get it over with, will you?"

She looked at him, guessing his thoughts, and said, "I know, I know."

"Take your time," he said. "It's OK." What a liar I am, he thought. She thinks she knows me.

Finally, she selected the egg-salad sandwich as he knew she would. She placed a pot of tea on her tray. She filled the small steel container with water out of the last urn, and looked at him, surprised. He could hear sighs behind him.

"Aren't you going to have anything?" she asked.

"Just a coffee," he said and filled a cup and put it on her tray.

"Aren't you going to eat *anything*?" Her brows knitted into furrows above her nose.

"No," he said and, glancing behind him at the guys in the lineup, he turned back to her and whispered, "We'd better get through here. People are waiting."

She rolled her eyes to the ceiling and shook her head, "I can't believe you sometimes, I really can't. You and your dad! It's enough to drive someone bonkers!"

He smiled lamely as she prepared to pay the cashier, but when the woman was half-way through, Shelley asked her if they had lemon wedges for the tea. The woman hesitated, sighed, then disappeared into the kitchen. He could hear the sighs behind him, too, or he thought he could. Lemon wedges, he thought, for Christ's sake end this! He couldn't believe her sometimes. There was always something else she wanted. Always one more thing. He couldn't stand it. Why don't you just take what you need, what's here, and be happy with it? Why do you always need something that isn't here, isn't right here in front of you? When the cashier came back from the kitchen, she had a lemon wedge on a small side dish and placed it next to the teapot.

"Thanks a lot," Shelley said, fishing in her purse for the change. Then, just as she'd settled up, just as they were moving out of the lineup, Shelley looked back at the woman and asked if she could get her a glass of fresh water. *Think of the people behind you!* he wanted to scream. But he didn't scream. He didn't say anything. After she got the water, they settled into a booth by the juke-box.

Shelley ate her egg-salad sandwich.

"It's good," she said, smiling across at him, "they used lots of mayonnaise and they've put onion in it, too. You'd like it. It's your style. It delivers."

He didn't laugh. He just said, "Terrific."

She looked over at him sitting there quietly and said, "I'm sorry about that comment."

"What comment?" he asked, avoiding her eyes.

"About you and your dad back there."

"Skip it," he said. "It was nothing."

"Well you know what I meant by it, don't you?"

"Of course I do," he said. "We've joked about it for years."

"Well, I'm sorry," she said. "It just bugs me sometimes."

"I know," he said.

He'd joked with his dad about it for years, too. He called it The Basil Fawlty Syndrome. Neil's father was shaky in a crisis and almost anything could cause a crisis. His otherwise patient and humorous side would give in to a side that was panicked, alert, exasperated. Neil's dad never wanted to be a bother. He couldn't stand taking up someone else's space. He couldn't impose on anyone or allow anyone to help him. He had to deal with everything swiftly, take up as little of anyone else's time as he could. Whenever he found himself in a queue, he'd get nervous, afraid he was going to put someone out. He'd lurch into a Basil Fawlty panic. One time, when he and Neil's mother had been in a Safeway Express Line, she'd pulled out a pile of coupons she'd put aside to save them money. She'd asked the teller to punch them in item by item, and his father had gone crazy. "*Think of the people behind you!*" he'd yelled and stomped out of the store shaking like a leaf. They'd all laughed about it for years and it had become his theme song. They'd whisper the words out to make him laugh. Sometimes it calmed him down

When Shelley had first met his dad, Neil had tried to explain. He blamed it on growing up poor in the depression in Nova Scotia, by being in the war overseas for five years, by raising a family on nothing in the fifties and sixties. But he knew it was deeper than those things.

It had something to do with how his dad saw things and cared about them, how his dad protected his inner life from people so that it was the one place he could be by himself and relax, where he didn't have to answer to anyone. There seemed very little in the outside world that matched his father's inner world. His dad dispensed with the outer world as quickly as possible, left few debts there so he could enter his inner world and sit there, satisfied, feeding on something he couldn't feed on in that other world because he couldn't believe it was there. Love.

Though his father's panic seemed a curious thing, it seemed natural, too. Neil felt that he understood. Words were the membrane that separated those two worlds and his dad seemed unable to find the words that would turn his inside world out. He could see him trying to do that sometimes when he'd been drinking, but most of the time Neil used a kind of semaphore to stay in touch with him. The semaphore was a humour his father felt relieved by.

That's why they loved *Fawlty Towers.* Basil was trapped behind a raging inarticulateness, too. He suffered the impositions of other people whining and whimpering at him, too. Basil was outrageous, and Neil's dad exulted in him. He'd laugh and laugh, and Neil would laugh with him. His dad loved stories in which some beleaguered underdog would rise up in the end and scream at all the pushy and competitive people around him, "Enough! There needs to be more gentleness in this world and I'm going to make you guys behave yourselves finally!" That was the key to it, Neil thought now, as he stared into his coffee cup while Shelley finished in the bathroom. His dad fed himself in an inner world because the world around him was so greedy, so selfish, so sure of itself. His father had been none of those things. He had a keen sense of the absurdity and gentleness in humans, and a seventh sense for a magic he believed humans capable of. No wonder he didn't expect anything. There was little out there that he wanted aside from his wife and children whom he didn't count as being out there. He'd wanted something else. Neil suspected sometimes that his father had found what he wanted, but it hadn't been easy for him. He'd suffered, too. In the end, he'd imploded into his silences, somewhere beyond the semaphore, and died.

The strange thing, Neil thought, is how much of his blood I have. That was why he dwelt on those crossings in his life when the two worlds faced one another and were the same thing. They were times he'd done something his dad hadn't been able to do. He'd discovered the words, the membranes that separated those worlds and by working really hard, he'd found he could live in both at the same time even. Yet when he'd stared down at the flat, waxen face of his father in the casket the night before the funeral, he became convinced that joining these worlds was futile, that each person was doomed to choose one or the other, never both. He looked up and saw Shelley walking back from the bathroom. She looked so full, so wonderful in the gold light that his heart turned over.

They'd loved one another for a long time. He wanted to lie in her arms and feel the connection, with everything, not just with her. But when she winked at him and jostled her purse over her shoulder, he had no idea who she was.

Neither of them talked when they were back out on the highway. Both were waiting for something to break.

She looked at him sideways every now and then. She saw his eyes and remembered the spark in them. She saw why she'd fallen in love with him in the first place: for his vitality, his thirst for things, the way he'd seemed so alive. She'd waited a long time to meet him. She'd gone through other lovers, but there had always been something else she wanted and he'd been that thing, the joy in him. She wanted it back, and as she stared out the window down to where Cochrane lay in the wide, green valley freckled with human homes, she wondered how far they would have to descend into his grief before they could surface whole again.

He knew she was stewing about what he'd said earlier. He couldn't blame her. What he'd said implied too much about their being together, about the confidence they had in one another. He knew that. He had to get out of the sorrow. It was frightening to think he could sink so far into it without being able to talk about it, or to think she was such a stranger to him suddenly. How could the mind play with the world so capriciously? How could it be so devious? What kind of a life was it where nothing could be sure, where things so valuable one moment could be swept away the next? Why was he even thinking these things and asking these questions? He was tired of the torture he was putting himself through, but he couldn't help it, it had always been like this with him. Christ! His nerves were as taut as the asphalt that stretched beneath them down the long hills into Canmore.

"Why don't we treat ourselves?" he said suddenly.

"What do you mean?"

"We're half an hour out of Banff," he said.

"So?"

"Well, why don't we stay overnight there?"

"It's so expensive!"

"I know, I know, but why don't we do it anyway? I'll put it on the Visa?"

"*Can* we put it on the Visa?"

"Sure we can."

"But what about work tomorrow?"

"I'll phone Brad from here. He'll understand."

"What about me?"

"I'll ask Brad to phone Mary. Don't worry. She'll understand, too. We'll get back Wednesday instead. No big deal."

"Well . . . "

"Come on!"

The motel on the strip was a nice place, as most of these places were. It had a queen size bed, a colour TV with loads of channels and options for movies, and an enormous bathroom with a jacuzzi. Shelley stretched her arms to the ceiling, and slipped off her shirt, eyeing the jacuzzi. Neither of them realized how tired they were.

He felt guilty about the luxury of the room. He always felt like that in these places, as if he were getting away with something, doing something other people could do but for some strange reason he couldn't. He didn't deserve it somehow. He might be getting away with it, but he felt awkward, furtive. He watched Shelley get out of her jeans and panties and start the water. How easily she accepted, even expected this situation while he felt so disarmed by it. What an inheritance, he sighed, as he walked down the thin, metal stairs onto the street. He was going for a coffee while she bathed. He'd bring back some takeout food so they could luxuriate on the bed and watch a movie.

Out on the main street he began to relax. The car had forced them too closely together. This was a good plan. He breathed in the smells of pine and cedar, and remembered these smells of Banff from his childhood.

Banff had always seemed a magic kingdom to him then, full of wonder. It had shimmered in colours and smells and excitement. It still does, he thought, as he took in all of the tourists milling about in their new clothes, excited, lost in holiday trances.

He gazed up at the far end of the street where the mountains rose so quietly. If you didn't look up, you could almost forget they were there. The vast mauve and grey stretches of rock fractured by sheaths of glacial snow were an astonishing contrast to the minute and contradictory human excitement beneath them. They just swept up, beginning in long stretches of green pine and cedar, and shredding eventually into heavy blocks of mauve rock bare and glistening in the sun. He stared up into the stately, quiet fissures in the stone, the cracks and thrusts of rock that created small dark shadows and crevices where, sometimes, he knew, tiny pockets of green survived high above the treeline, separated from the thicker growth at the base below.

The street was full of motion, colour, voices, signs and shops. The cars whisked by, people jostled one another in that friendly, hopeful way tourists adopted as they walked to shops or sights listed in brochures. Nothing fit together down here in the street unless the swirl itself was a thing. And he guessed it was, in the end, something in itself.

The almost solemn quiet of those stretches of stone again; the endless motion surrounding him on the sidewalk. He could hold them both in his head.

It was going to be all right.

The long sorrow that was closing in on him, rising and falling in his chest, became incarnate.

It was incredible. It was his father folding him in a soft laugh. Boy, he whispered to himself, it's painful and shitty and long and arduous, but when this thing pays off, Dad, it sure delivers! He looked up into the green and grey rock again, grateful, tired.

"Are you all right?" someone near him asked.

He shook his head, regaining the street. "Oh yes," he apologized. "I'm fine, fine. Sorry."

"Are you sure?"

"Oh yes. Sorry. I didn't mean to bother you. I am fine! *Really!*"

He moved away quickly until he lost his audience, then slowed down, taking it all in again. He clenched his fists in an exquisite surety. This was what he expected: it was everything, it was that big. Whatever else happened, you had to put yourself right here, in the crease between them.

As she wrapped herself around him in the darkness, she knew he would be all right. The light in his eyes was back. She knew he'd been right when he'd said what he said in the car, but he'd also been wrong. As they laughed and groaned into one another in the dark, she pulled his face down to hers suddenly and giggled up into it, "Come on! Hurry!"

"What do you mean?" he whispered back, surprised.

She drew his ear down to her lips and laughed, "Think of the people behind you!"

Taste

They didn't know a soul in Strasbourg. Neither of them could speak French. They assumed they'd just arrive by train from London and snap up an apartment. They'd been told everyone in Strasbourg could speak fluent English. Dead wrong. Wrong, wrong, wrong.

They were sitting in their sun-filled apartment in the midst of their new morning ritual. Rick watched Jennifer's thumbs ease into the thin crust of the croissant, breaking it inside out to expose fragile layers of white dough unfolding in an endless succession of delicate membranes. It reminded him of something. It's much like a flower, he thought. Yeah, a flower. A rose. Sure.

He remembered the weight he'd lost the first week when they'd struggled to rent an apartment through an *agent immoblier,* the only way you could rent an apartment in Strasbourg. He'd had to mime his way through the most complicated set of legal contracts he'd ever seen. The French had invented bureaucracy all right. He'd been so tense — the renting of the apartment, the hooking up of the utilities, the straightening out of their visas at the Prefecteur — he'd shed fifteen pounds. No one would have believed him back home. In the end, they'd rented a small, one-room apartment in Petite France. They'd furnished it sparsely from a department store in Place Des Halles, and, within a week, had begun to feel at home a bit. He'd still sit up late at night in the kitchen with the door closed, smoking, making cup after cup of coffee, worrying about whether they'd make it. They were both "nesters" and place meant everything. But the key was to ritualize this new place and that's why each morning he'd get up, make a small pot of coffee, go down onto the cobblestone street and get smokes at the Tabac shop, croissants at the *pattisserie,* and a pint of milk at the *cremerie.* On the third morning, just as he'd rounded the corner of St. Pierre Le Jeune Cathedral and headed east up Le Grand Rue, the sun broke over the cobblestone streets in startling shards of gold. The shopkeepers on Le Grand Rue were hosing dogshit off the pavement. The smell of the cool water on the stones and the gold of the sun dancing into it made Rick feel exhilarated, at home. Isn't it strange that something this concrete, this random, could save you in the end while nothing in your mind could.

"Boy-oh-boy!" Jennifer held the croissant aloft in both hands, then drew it up to her mouth and took a bite. "It's incredible," she sighed, rolling her eyes upward, grinning at him in spite of her cheeks and her mouth churning with it. "Just incredible!"

"That's *incroyable!*" he whispered from his chair. "The word is *incroyable!*"

"Whatever," she sighed, ignoring him. She was too busy negotiating another approach. It wasn't easy to do. There's a skill, he knew, and it has to do with the crumbs. She'll master it, whatever it is. She always had before. He avoided croissants because of his beard. He'd already embarrassed them one morning in a café just after they'd first arrived. But she worshipped them. In fact, the early morning ritual of croissants had saved her. He was sure of it. It's one of the reasons she's not afraid to stay here now. Rituals are like that.

Both of them were already working. She painted in the living room, which was also the bedroom. She'd spread out her paints and watercolour paper on an eight foot length of plywood he'd mounted on two aluminum sawhorses. The wide windows above this table flung open, so she painted in the fresh air and looked down on an enclosed garden that sat, squared, beneath all the other apartment windows. She had to be careful not to leave the windows open when she was finished for the pigeons would come right in and sit down on the desk, making themselves at home.

He worked in the tiny kitchen. He moved the table they ate at from the living room into the kitchen every morning and placed it squarely in front of the kitchen sink and window, typing. The problem was that while he was doing this they couldn't open the fridge or get into the bathroom. If they needed either of these things, he'd have to move. It was close quarters but they put up with it and began to feel industrious, almost innocent. It's hard to account for, he thought.

He watched her as she placed the plate on the floor, took a sip of her coffee, then rose up, stretching, pulling off her nightshirt over her shoulders. As she leaned down to select her clothes from the makeshift cupboard, her breasts fell forward like fruit and her legs shone over the thin broadloom. He considered this feast, then looked out the window, modest. Something was happening to them here and he couldn't explain it. They'd been together for fourteen years, since she'd been nineteen and he twenty-six. They'd been through everything together, he'd thought, but he'd been wrong.

Today was a reward. Neither of them was going to work. They'd been at it for five days straight and had designated today as a break. We have even gone so far, he reminded himself uneasily, we don't know what we'll do or where we'll go.

She appeared before him, fresh from the shower, her hair blown back by the hairdryer. She stood in the kitchen doorway, her hands on her hips, smirking at him. "Oooh la la!" he whispered. She was wearing a loose cotton blouse with its top buttons undone. She wasn't wearing a bra, and the outlines of her breasts were visible through the opening at the top of her blouse and in the shadows cast beneath the white cotton. Not wearing a bra was unheard of for her. It was why he'd said what he'd said. The blouse was tucked into a short blue skirt she'd bought the day before, the closest thing to a miniskirt he'd seen in ages. He'd been surprised when she'd bought it. She'd always been a bit reserved in her outfits. It was just the way she was. It's the French influence. She was picking up on their taste.

The women in Strasbourg dressed to kill. He'd only seen flair like this years ago when he'd spent a few days in Montreal. It really was *incroyable*. And here Jennifer stood before him, dressed to kill, too. He wondered suddenly whether she was wearing any panties under the skirt, and almost laughed out loud at how funny the wondering seemed to him. It, too, was uncharacteristic. Maybe I'm turning into a typical Frenchman. Maybe I'm changing, too. "You look fantastic!" he said before she began to consider his chuckling and misinterpret it. If there was even a small chance her outfit seemed funny to him, she'd change it, and he didn't want her to. He locked the door and they descended into the dark, through three floors of circular stairs, hand in hand. Because of the thick dark, they had to squint into the bright spring gold of the tiny streets of Petite France. They breathed in the lilac air, the crisp April breeze, and let their clothes flap delicately against their skin.

Rick and Jennifer walked up the cobblestone past the square at Maison Des Tanneurs where all the tiny tables and chairs had been set out since the weather had turned warm. They walked past the towering rose stone of St. Thomas Cathedral, through the small enclosed streets that fed Rue Des Peches, and out onto the *Quai* that circled the city in a network of wide canals that reminded him of photographs of Venice he'd seen in books.

Out on the *Quai* the people of Strasbourg were walking their dogs, or sitting in groups on tiny green enamel benches. Street artists were painting and hawking small scenes, beggars begging, lovers necking or walking hand in hand, or practically making love right there on the stones.

At first they'd been disarmed by how physical the people of Strasbourg were. Rick and Jennifer were Canadians, after all, and had grown up in their heads. They'd look away when they spotted a middle-aged couple necking at a bus stop, or a young couple fondling one another, stretched flat out on a bench or on the grass by the canal. They were getting used to this outward affection now, though, and it was a good thing, for it was unavoidable. Initially, they'd wondered whether it hadn't surfaced artificially because it was spring, but in time they accepted it was what happened here all the time: a vibrance of bodies, as outward as the streets, the shops, the color, all the bright red and blue geraniums bursting out of green pots along the *Quai* in the windowsills of tiny apartments. Old women leaned out of the windows and smiled right back at them as they walked by. Sometimes, the whole place pulsed in a physical life he'd never sensed before, anywhere.

Their first stop was at a small café on Rue Des Juifs, tucked away behind the main cathedral, lost on one of the many sidestreets. The city's streets had grown in a circular pattern because of the canals, and the pattern had grown labyrinthine over the centuries. You'd never find this café, he knew, unless you memorized the maze that concealed it. Its two waitresses had gotten to know them, asking and answering questions in English. Jennifer ordered a slice of apple-crisp that had an exotic French name, and he ordered a bowl of *café au lait* and a piece of walnut pie, the most delicious pie he'd ever tasted. As he lifted the fork to his lips, he could see, out of the corner of his eye, just above the fork, three dazzling young students prance by holding one another's hands and giggling. One of them winked at him when she spotted him watching. He winked back, then laughed at himself for doing it. "Who were you winking at?" Jennifer asked around the mouthful of apple-crisp she'd slipped off her fork. He told her what had happened, then wrapped his mouth around the walnut pie, his tongue savouring the caramel sauce that held the walnuts together.

They walked west on the Rue Des Juifs, passing a small market that had, as its feature display, a table of fresh, red strawberries pointing their bright heads up into the sun and shade of the square. While the vendor and his girlfriend necked on a green chair at the back of the stall, Rick and Jennifer drew up to examine the strawberries. Though there were thousands on display, someone had arranged them meticulously, so typical of everything in Strasbourg. Presentation was crucial, they'd learned, and the strawberries had been sculpted in piles that rose up out of the green crate like tiny, polished pyramids. Each strawberry was the size of small lemons back home, and their deep red surfaces shone like roses in the sun. When they bought a bag of them, the vendor grinned broadly, conspiratorily. As Rick and Jennifer walked away, he returned to his girlfriend who was waiting, smiling, behind the display, her lips the colour of the strawberries sitting like a field in front of her.

They snuck up on the main cathedral from behind, from the east.

When they'd arrived in Strasbourg, on their first morning, they'd walked out of the Hotel Europe and stumbled onto Notre Dame Cathedral from the intended direction for tourists, from the west. It had been built to present itself to the west. Its seven hundred foot façade towered over the cobblestone square beneath it and its famous Western Rose Window shined its triumph out to the citizens and tourists who stood day after day in the square below, necks craned upward. Neither Rick nor Jennifer had expected anything so wondrous. In the brochures on Strasbourg they'd pored over back home, the Notre Dame Cathedral was always emphasized, but they'd had no idea just how beautiful it would turn out to be. It stretched its endless gothic intricacy up over the square; there was no place the eye could rest because the baroque intensity of the carvings in the embellished rose stone never ended, never stopped presenting more nuances not noticed before. On that first morning the two of them had stood there, spellbound. They'd wondered, even then, what they'd done right to deserve such a gift. Now, three months later, they were sneaking up behind it, their old friend, behind its dark, long side-naves that cantilevered onto the streets. They sat down in one of their favorite outdoor cafés beneath the cathedral, La Glace Place, and ordered espressos and small dishes of Italian ice cream served in tiny, silver serving bowls.

As he sat there staring up at the stone façade that laced the air above them, as the people of Strasbourg milled around him in bright-coloured clothes and smiles and shouts and stares, Rick looked over at Jennifer while she was looking away at a kiosk of postcards. He noticed the sharp line of the cotton against the pink of her breast, the rustle of her long, slender legs as she shuffled them back and forth beneath the checkered tablecloth: this woman he had fallen in love with years ago when they'd both been so much younger. He saw her with new eyes, as if he'd just met her over there, perhaps, in front of the *papeterie* where she bought her supplies.

His new eyes were the eyes of his body.

He was staring at how her hair brushed her ear in strands that moved delicately with the slow pivoting motion of her head. He saw her eyes taking things in, soft hazel orbs looking out at the world filled with a wonder they'd never stopped feeling here. He could see a vein in her neck throbbing with blood. He flicked his eyes down to the left and saw his own hand spread out flat on the checkered tablecloth. It was a web of skin and vein over bone, and it moved and curled when he willed it to. He could feel both the sun and the shade on his hand when he moved it across the table. Heat and cold. He looked up again at her and saw her lips open slightly, then close. Here they were, then, the two of them, he thought. They were both alive. They were both going to die. This was their time, their blood. He splayed his fingers out on the tablecloth and watched them move again. He regarded her lips in the sun. He could feel the weight of his feet as they brushed the cobblestone beneath them. The stones were smooth and round and cool in the shade. He flicked off his sandal so he could feel them more clearly with his toes. He regarded her lips. They opened slightly, then closed. Jennifer was breathing. The cotton of the tablecloth felt sacred beneath his fingertips. He gulped air into his mouth, astonished, afraid.

Incarnation, his body whispered back at his fear.

He groaned inwardly at the rush of it, as if he were a flower opening to the air it loves for the first time, tasting the world tasting it.

Rick looked at Jennifer more fiercely, hoping she might anchor him. He felt wondrous, adrift, unsafe. She smiled back at him.

All afternoon they wandered through the sidestreets of the downtown maze. They loved being out here now, where all the people were. They loved the communal street feeling of it compared to the closed houses and televisions back home. They felt part of something physical. They grinned into the sun overhead, bought a bouquet of flowers from a vendor in Place Kleber, and decided to buy a small box of Strasbourg chocolates for later, too. Finally, as they circled back to Petite France, they picked up the cream and a baguette of French bread. Lugging the packages with them, they ascended the dark stairs of the apartment building and unlocked the door.

Jennifer spread a fresh, blue-checkered cloth on the table. She set the open box of chocolates at the back, and in the centre a huge white bowl of strawberries after she'd rinsed them in the sink. Next to them she set a small bowl of cream. Beside this she placed two tiny eating bowls and spoons that shone in the afternoon sun flickering through the window. Finally, at the front of the table, a bit to the side, she arranged the bouquet of flowers in a coffee mug so the colors could catch the sun.

They stood there, staring at what she'd done, mystified. He faced her and held her in his arms. She gazed up at him and they kissed: a long, slow kiss as they'd kissed when they'd first met. They began to undress one another. He removed her blouse by unbuttoning it button by button, then slipping it off her round, soft shoulders. Her breasts played light and shadow before him in the undulating light from the window. She removed his teeshirt and began to undo his belt. As each item of clothing joined the others on the floor, he felt as if he was watching from a distance while another part of him, a part he hadn't known before, had taken over. And instead of resisting it this time, instead of guarding his fear of it, he gave in.

They sat cross-legged, facing one another, on the bed. She stood up in time and brought over the bowl of strawberries. They ate them one by one, dipping each one in the cream, then wrapping their lips around the swollen red fruit. After they'd finished the strawberries, they ate the chocolates one by one, too.

The sun descended around them through the open window, and the light in the room faded and washed their bodies in a gold sigh. Finally, with the gentle chucking sounds of the pigeons roosting close by on the window-ledges, and the farther, muted whisper of the street below singing its small spring song, he tasted her for the first time.

Roofs in the Sun

They fulfilled some romantic fantasy he guessed, a buried memory of Medieval Europe manufactured from books borrowed from The Bookmobile during those -35° C Edmonton winters when he was a boy. His imagination must have been fueled by medieval village scenes, especially scenes that represented the architecture of those times, those tiled roofs, because when he first saw them, it was like a homecoming. One month after they'd arrived in Strasbourg, a woman named Christiane offered them the use of her Peugot for a month, and the first thing they'd done was head up into The Vosges, into those roofs.

Andlau, west of Obernai, was a small village tucked into a pass that fed cities like Nancy in the next valley of Eastern France. On the narrow road up, through pines that brushed the asphalt they were so pendulous with snow, they'd had their first glimpse of Alsatian villages and their soft rose roofs shining in the air. There was something about the roofs that intrigued and comforted him though he couldn't put a name to either. He couldn't get over them. Splashed against predictable landscapes that were much like the Okanagan Valley, were the unpredictable textures of old stone houses capped by thick, tiled roofs. He discovered later that the tiles were red because of the clay of the Alsace, and that up in Lorraine, for example, or small cities south of Paris like Joigny, the roofs were cream-coloured or grey from different mineral deposits in the soil. But there was something about his first sighting of the red tiled roofs of Andlau that he couldn't get over, that he kept with him for years.

They'd pulled up onto the curb on the main street. It had snowed earlier, but now there was a fine rain falling, covering the stone and tiles in a brilliant veneer of water. He walked into a *patisserie* for two takeout coffees. While he was waiting, he glanced out the huge plate-glass window at the front of the store, over the rows of *tartes l'oignon* and peach flans, past her face grinning back at him from the passenger side of the car, up to the surface of a romanesque church with its bleached rose stone, past the roof of the church up into the trees that fell away from it on the mountainside above and, there, hundreds of shiny red roofs glistening in the rain. As far as he could see, up near the top of the mountain, a patch of these roofs shone like diamonds in a sun winking only there, above the clouds shrouding the town below. He felt transported, as if life was something that breathed in a dark enclosure of heavy drapes that brushed the floor around him until, abruptly, in the middle of the most ordinary, petty passage, the drapes would open for no reason and disclose parts of a wonder before they closed again, quickly and thickly.

He climbed back into the car and handed her a coffee. An elderly woman shuffled past the *patisserie* and smiled at them for no reason. The ashtray was full. The hazard lights clicked rhythmically through the silence . . .

Roofs in the Morning

It's not easy to explain because when I try it always sounds like something else when it isn't. There is an intimacy about neighbourhoods early in the morning that only occurs then, when the sun is just beginning to catch the roofs and the chimneys, when the street is so quiet only non-habitual sounds, like a car driving by, or the backing-up beep of a delivery truck a couple of blocks away, draw attention to themselves and break the sense of a cocoon unfolding in the morning air, a cocoon that is a collective rather than an individual thing.

It's the collective nature of it that intrigues me and makes me wonder, for it flies in the face of the privacy that defines neighbourhoods: all the obvious grids and lines drawn round a person — the curbs, fences, garages, garbage cans, curtains, doors with latches — that defy collectivity and persist as quiet announcements of borders in the air. Maybe it's the relaxation of these borders early in the morning beneath these roofs that creates the intimacy I'm thinking of this morning. I'm not sure. It's just that this intimacy is almost physical and, in some curious ways, accessible, whatever that means. On another level, I guess, this intimacy and its collective nature redeems other things that happen to us.

We're down here in Vancouver for a few days staying in her brother's flat on the main floor of an old house on West Twelfth in Kitsilano. If you're familiar with Vancouver, his flat is just south of Broadway, a couple of blocks down from the futuristic McDonald's, west of the Hollywood theater and east of Orestes Restaurant. You know where I am, then.

We're down here because she has an appointment with her specialist and we're trying to make the trip simple and inexpensive by staying in his flat and avoiding the West End where we'd be tempted to spend money. We put Malcolm on the plane this morning, the morning after we arrived, so we have his place to ourselves now, which is nice in another way, too. The privacy I was talking about earlier, I guess.

He's off to Ecuador for six weeks with a friend. He's excited about it and, naturally, we got caught up in the excitement. We pored over his atlas with him, browsed through his guide books, listened to the itinerary that had been set up for him by a travel agent. It was fascinating to be drawn into a landscape, suddenly, that I was completely unaware of except in general terms like the vague, solid shape of South America itself in my mind. Also, because this is a new flat for him, we were drawn into its details for the first time and that was fun, too.

It's a small, two-bedroom flat renovated in the early eighties. The owner of the house had raised the house twelve feet, poured a basement, then finished it off as a rental to pay down the mortgage.

It's a very Kitsilano thing to do. Everywhere you look in this neighbourhood, no matter how small the house, you become aware of its division into rental flats. In some ways, these neighbourhoods have at least double, maybe triple the residents they might have had back in the twenties and thirties when they were all single family dwellings.

After we put him on the plane this morning, we drove around the city a bit, went for a cappuccino in a small café on West Fourth, then picked up some bagels for supper. Because her appointment is for tomorrow, we decided to stay at home tonight and go out for supper and a movie tomorrow night when the appointment is behind her and we don't feel so distracted. We're thinking of seeing a new flick called *The Crying Game*. It's supposed to be good. It's supposed to have a plot twist, like *Body Heat*. You can never tell in advance. You just hope that's true. But staying home tonight was a good move. She and I both love bagels but don't get to eat them much because nobody makes good bagels back in Vernon. We bought some cream cheese, sliced some tomatoes and sat and talked and watched the television for a while. Both of us had trouble getting to sleep. We had a lot on our minds, I guess. Things have built up over the past three months while she's been sick. She's in remission now, though, and her visit to her specialist will confirm it, we think, and allow her, both of us I guess, to breathe a bit more easily. But you can't tell about these things in advance either. We've made these trips before and both of us are drifting in and out of those memories, positive and negative. At one point, while neither of us could sleep, we talked more honestly than we ever had about sickness, about hope and the things that interfere with it. It was a painful talk in some ways. The darkness allowed both of us to be more direct than we usually are, to abandon some of the protectiveness we use to shield ourselves from things. We cried and became even closer in the dark, an incredible thing considering the first trip we made like this one was in 1975, seventeen years ago. Then she fell asleep. I watched her for a while then got up and sat on the couch in his living room. I played with his radio tuner trying to get CBC but mostly getting Seattle stations instead. Something to do with his cable channels, I guessed. That, and living so close to Seattle.

But tuning in the Seattle stations was fascinating by itself. Listening to the early deejays talk about local traffic patterns there made me feel like a voyeur, as if I was peering in on a closed, ritualized world of early morning coffee and cars in the mist and ferry schedules. It wasn't like listening to your own station. It really did feel like another world, another country. Finally, around 6:00 AM I found the CBC and lay on the couch listening to the morning show, its familiar voices and announcements. I showered eventually and decided to go out for a coffee and bring her home something from a bakery for breakfast.

Out on the street in the early sun, it was cold. This is an unusual cold snap for Vancouver and you actually have to scrape the windows and let the car warm up for ten minutes before setting out. If I don't wait, my Tercel will stall, and sometimes when it stalls it will flood itself and it can take another fifteen or twenty minutes to get it going again. It wasn't really built for weather this cold. So I scraped the window and sat in the car, watching. While I did this other people surfaced to warm their cars and I could see still more moving in windows while dozens of lights came on.

One young man in a blue parka with the hood up so that fur circled his head, came out on the street across from me and scraped off the windows of an old Dodge truck, then sat in it and turned it over, sitting there just like me. I nodded at him and he flashed a wide smile back. I could see his teeth, white in the grey haze of the window above the dash. I imagined him tuning in his favourite station on the radio or even flicking a cassette in. On the other side of the street a woman in her late twenties was standing in her living room window in her housecoat, holding a cup of coffee in both hands. I could see the veins moving in the hand facing me. Her head was tilted upwards. She was looking at something behind and above my car. A young girl in blue pajamas joined her eventually, squinted out directly at me, then dragged her mother off by pulling her housecoat. They disappeared into a bright light that must have been in the kitchen at the back of the house. Two cars passed me, both gauging the ruts in the road so they wouldn't come too close to my car. I kept thinking, they do this every morning. The only thing different about this one is that I'm sitting here, a strange face, a strange car. Sitting in the dawn.

Every morning, I thought. And I wondered about their lives, the surfaces of the arborite counters in their kitchens, the feel of their boots as they slipped into them, the brush of nylon against arms and legs as they dressed for the cold. I wondered about their coffees, their orange juice, their different breakfasts, and the dishes they left on the table or cleaned up and put away. I could almost see the different wallpaper and rugs. And each of these people, if I had eye contact with them, was open, smiling, in the strange freedom and hopefulness faces acquire in the morning for some reason. I don't know, but it seemed I was slipping into the physical texture of the lives around me, fabric for fabric, flesh for flesh. And I almost wanted to be there every morning with them, be part of this breathing. I wanted everything, I guess. Love is like that, isn't it? Then I saw her standing in her brother's window, waving back at me, trying to get my attention, pointing dramatically at the mug of coffee she was holding out with one hand, and I thought this is my morning, she is my morning, here where I've found myself lost again, the vague, solid shape of it . . .

The Bright Field

Back to where
I could heal all the air
I ever spoke through, and have
nobody thinking about me, ever.

— Don Coles, "The Artist's Brother,"
Forests Of The Medieval World

There's sudden pleasure as his eyes consume the early morning blue of the window above the sewing machine, and his cheeks feel the soft breeze shuffling through the window's aluminum frames. A pleasure just for the eyes, it seems, and he wonders vaguely why something is not going wrong in all this. An old reflex of his almost swims to the surface of this wondering, but it dives back down into him again while his mind claims this world above the surface of the normal. There is something he is sure of now, though he can't give it a name. He can feel his heart racing to meet this certainty, and his body trembles in the pleasure of the meeting. Sure. You bet. Absolutely. And he is aware, in an odd sideways fashion, of the tiny cotton rolls on the blanket he's pulled up to his chin in the night, and of his legs twitching beneath the blanket. He feels he doesn't have to move, and this feels wonderful, this need not to have to jump up into anything.

Their mother wandered in from the kitchen, wiping her hands on her apron. She sat down in the rose chair at the far end of the room, completing the circle they made. "What are you arguing about *now,* for heaven's sake?"

"We're wondering about that summer we were driving back from Nova Scotia, and we ended up in that corn field," Jane sighed and grinned at her two younger brothers. "Remember that afternoon Mom? Dad talked about it so often."

"But I wasn't there," their mother announced.

"No, you stayed back in the campground," Rick said.

"Yeah, you were making chile for supper, remember?" Neil added.

"Glory, that's right!" their mother laughed. "That was my famous campfire chile!"

"Yeah," Rick whispered, staring away from his mother, shaken suddenly, removed.

Their mother pulled her legs up under her knees and settled back into the chair. "But what is it you want to know?"

They were all tired, but not tired enough to stop talking about their father. It was as if they couldn't rest until they'd talked him into the ground they'd laid him into the day before. When the six Legionnaires had stood so stiffly in the spring air. When the bugle had blown those notes high up into the sky above the brown casket. As if something hadn't been completed in those notes. Something that had to be named before they could sleep.

He's being protected from something. He's sure of it. His eyes are focusing beyond the blue window, through the wire mesh of the screen, and it feels so good doing this, simply, and he has a feeling that if he breaks his stare through the window, something else will happen, something darker and not so good. And, as he passes through the vagueness of this wonder, he sees her standing there, through the blue in the window. It's his mother and she's standing in the blue flower-printed dress she always wears in summer. He can see the outlines of the caragana hedge behind her head, but he's concentrating on her face, the deep smile in her eyes, her arms stretching out towards him. Yes, they are stretching out towards him and he can remember, even though it doesn't feel like a memory — this clear image in the blue of the window, her face — he can remember his boy-self running up towards her with his fishing rod in his hand. Yes, I've been fishing below Greenhill Lookout and I haven't caught a thing. He laughs now, feels his cheeks crease into the white cotton of the pillow, and, as he thinks about the pillow, the difference between the grain of the fabric on the pillow and the soft skin of his mother's cheeks, he realizes that the image in the blue of the window has changed and now it's Colette standing there in her war suit, her arms stretching out towards him, too. He can see just a bit of the sign above her head in the background. It's the 'GOW' of New Glasgow, and Colette is standing in the railway station that time just after he'd been released from the Army. He'd been staying with his mother, in Westville. That's right, and Colette had written to him from Moncton. He's laughing into the pillow again, laughing so hard he feels the tears dampening the cotton. She had written to say that if he met her at the station in New Glasgow then she'd know he was serious after all those stupid letters from overseas, or, if he didn't meet her there then she'd accept he'd never been serious, just a soldier writing letters, just a loneliness over there that needed all those words to her, all those promises he'd meant, sitting in jeeps or small squares in those villages when he'd had the time to write her. And here he is now running towards her so she'll know he'd meant those things about the future, about the children they'd have who would run towards them one day with big smiles and hearts on their sleeves. Isn't this wonderful, he sighs. Something important is happening here, isn't it, but all I can do is stare and laugh and cry. There's a stillness here, in the weight of my feet that cannot move, my breath that's rising to meet the blue of the window, her face smiling, all framed in aluminum. It's soft and lovely to lie here and not have to move, not have to say anything at all.

"Well," Rick said, "You're the eldest, Jane. You go first."

"For what it's worth, then," Jane began, "I think dear old Dad was happy in that field that afternoon because we were almost back to Edmonton and he knew he'd be picking up his old routines in a couple of days."

"He hadn't been drinking all summer, though, remember *that*!" Rick interrupted.

"Oh I know that . . . " Jane said, "I haven't forgotten that, Rick. It's really the point of what I'm saying, though. He *hadn't* been drinking all summer but he knew he could pick it up again, soon, and he must have felt good about that, excited about it."

"But that's not how it works all the time," Rick whispered.

"What do you mean," Jane looked at him, "*that's not how it works?*"

"Not always." Rick spoke very softly. "You know that."

The old house sits in the distance in the square blue of the window and he's approaching it somehow. The old house when it was new, when they'd first bought it. There's no lawn yet and a wooden sidewalk runs from the gravel across the muddy yard, and up to the porch steps where they're all sitting, waving, and looking up at something above his head. Colette, Jane, Neil and Rick, all sitting or standing now, waving at him, smiling. He realizes this is the day they moved in. Frank had dropped the four of them off at the house while he'd spent the day at the apartment on 124th Street packing up their things. It's late now, and he and Frank are pulling up in the truck with all their stuff, and the four of them are sitting on the porch, waiting, excited. It's beautiful to see their faces shining up at him because he's there. It's lovely, isn't it, and when he opens his eyes, it's the house again, but this time he's standing in front of it, holding a car door open. Jane, Rick and Neil are bounding down the stairs, across the lawn and the cement sidewalk, in their summer clothes, excited. Colette is standing behind the wire mesh of the front screen door, smiling at him. This is the day I bought the car finally, he thinks, the old Hillman, and I'm taking the kids down to Frosty Inn for cones. He closes his eyes again and remembers the three of them asking him endless questions about the car while they eat their ice creams: how much a used car costs, what the buttons are for, how fast it can go, whether they could drive out to a lake in it. Wonderful, their faces excited, leaning into his confidence, and this gift that sits, squat and heavy on the gravel like a chalice. And, suddenly, there's the house again, in winter. Enormous piles of snow lie on either side of the walk. They're all at the door this time, waving. He is lugging a TV he's rented for Christmas up the wooden stairs, and the kids are like Mexican jumping beans they're so excited. Colette is smiling quietly behind them in a green-flowered dress, her arms folded beneath her breasts, her head moving from side to side, gently. He closes his eyes to hold all of them standing there looking up at him, the thickness of it, the stillness of it again, and he feels the warmth of the tears on the pillow and his cheeks creasing into the cotton in a wide smile for the stillness of the holding of them in his eyes.

Rick was smiling and crying at the same time, rubbing his forehead with his left hand, embarrassed. Neil was standing at the window while Jane knelt in front of Rick, holding his right hand in both of hers. Their mother sat quietly in the rose chair, waiting, uneasy, disarmed.

"Well, I don't know," Rick said, smiling up into Jane's face. "I've thought about it for years. It's just that he was so calm. He wasn't in his usual, I don't know . . . "

"Basil Fawlty panic?" Neil suggested.

"Exactly," Rick said. "He wasn't twitching around, exasperated, blowing his fuse at every turn of the screws. In fact, he was the opposite and that's why we all get stuck. He was standing there, his arms folded — not smoking either if you remember precisely — and smiling and watching us as we ran through those corn stalks. It was eerie, looking back on it. We all wondered then why he didn't get us out of there, say something like 'You can't run through here like a bunch of crazed banshees for Christ's sake!' But he didn't. He didn't say anything. And he seemed happy. Genuinely happy in that relaxed way you could see in other people, but never in him. I think it was because he hadn't been drinking, and, for once, even though he picked it up again as soon as we got back, for once he was just healthy enough, just free enough of all the shit and guilt he lived with most of the time, that he was caught, surprised, by a calmness that could have become him, I guess, that in some ways was the Charles we never saw. Do you know what I mean? It's crazy, but that's what I think took hold of him that afternoon. He was ambushed by an accident of calmness he wasn't used to, or didn't expect."

"I like that version," Neil said. "It would be nice to think of him being caught off guard like that. And maybe you're right. Maybe you're right. When I think of him standing there like that, looking at us, I guess I wonder whether it wasn't money and time that didn't cause that sudden calm. I don't know, but I guess I wonder whether he wasn't simply relaxed because we'd gotten through the summer for once without him having to spend the whole time working at Northlands, at the track. Because we'd driven down to Nova Scotia, he'd actually had the summer off for once. And because we'd rented out the house while we were gone, we were actually going to have the money to get through September without borrowing scads of cash. And that seldom happened. We were always broke in August and still had over a month to go before he'd be paid. So, for once, he could stand there and actually enjoy something without having his mind racing over all sorts of scams he'd have to invent to get by Mom and get us through. All that scheming, all those normal lies he had to mount up and run. In my mind, I see him there, surprised too, but by something working out for once, a huge burden being lifted off of him. I don't know, but that's how I see him there."

"Well, I wasn't there so I wouldn't know," their mother said. She was leaning back in the chair, one hand adjusting the curls on the side of her head. She was tired, but still talking. "Life was never easy for your father, and you all sound right to me. All of those things were true. Each of them." She lifted her legs out from beneath her and sat straight up in the chair, leaning her elbows down on her knees, holding her hands together. "Your dad's mind was so complicated that all those things could be happening at once in it. Really! More even. That's how his mind worked." She laughed suddenly, and stared into her hands flexing on her knees. "I couldn't figure him out, dears, and I lived with him for forty-two years for pity's sake! Think about that!" Her face lit up at her own humour. "He was always too shifty, too complicated. I'd push him and push him, to try and get in there, but it wasn't easy with him, never easy." She started to cry softly and all three converged on her chair.

"Oh dear," their mother sobbed, "when I think of him sometimes. When I think of how hard things were for him." She rocked forward and back, the tears coming silently. "But when I found him there, dears?" She looked up at Jane, then sideways to both of her sons. "His cough was so bad that he slept in the guest room. That was what we always did when his cough was bad like that. He'd go in there so we could both get some sleep. Or, at least, I could. And it was Sunday night remember, so he was out of gin which meant he was not only coughing, but shaky, too. When I woke up in the morning and passed the room and he was so quiet, I wondered right away, didn't I? I wondered why he was so quiet, why I couldn't hear him like I usually could."

He can sense the car cooling off on the gravel road behind him. It's the '56 Meteor, the blue one. He knows it's there somehow. That's such a good car, he smiles to himself, and as he smiles he opens his eyes again and can see it all so clearly in the frame of the window. He can see it all so clearly that he forgets about the frame and falls forward into the scene itself. Oh, the yellow and green of the tall corn stalks against the deep blue of the North Dakota sky. It's here, he thinks suddenly as his heart accelerates, it's here in the field.

"Well, there he was, lying on his side. His eyes were open and he was staring out the window. There was a breeze rustling through the window. The screen was open. He always liked that, getting the fresh air in. And the sky was that clear blue it always is in the spring here. You know. And his left hand was drawn up and clenched right at his heart. Right at his heart! You could see the veins in his hand popping, it was clenched so tightly. And his other arm, his right arm, was stretched out from the bed, like his fingers were pointing at something in the window. And oh!" she cried suddenly, her sobs a sound now, "he was so still, and I was afraid. I was so afraid standing there by myself. And I knew he was gone. I didn't have to touch him to know that."

He feels he's in the middle of a huge puzzle and is just about to fit the last piece into it when there, in the midst of the stalks to his right, he sees Jane's face peeping out at him, laughing. "Hi Dad!" she yells, then disappears. Now, on his left, Rick's face, "It's me, Dad! It's me!" vanishing as quickly into the bold and thick yellow all around him. And now, astonishingly, right before him, it's Neil's smile staring up at him, "Hello dere!", and gone like magic, like a wand had been waved. He can hear them rustling. He can't see them, but he hears their small bodies racing through the stalks. He hears them stumbling and hooting and falling all over the place, laughing helplessly at nothing but this abandoned glee provided by a simple corn field in the summer sun. He can hold the mystery for once. These are my children, and these are their lives rustling and growing around me in the blue air. I can't see them but I can hold them in here. I can hold my heart open like this, open to the sun, turning it inside out to the yellow and the blue and, oh!, it feels so graceful, and he is aware of his eyes squinting into the corner of the pillow, of his unshaven cheeks drawing up then down against the fabric of the cotton. He is wondering how they actually make cotton when he opens his eyes into the yellow and the blue again, and his ears into his children's invisible laughing and rustling, and he feels his heart open even more suddenly. It's Colette and she is standing as surely behind him as the car is sitting there, cooling off in the sun. And, abruptly, he feels it's all here, everything is complete, moving in a wild shuffling that never ends but is also still, able to be held and breathed as one thing, and he can see in the blue sky above the field the sun turn into a black ball that grows suddenly larger. Now, slowly, as he looks at it with all these other things folding outward in his eyes, the black ball becomes as thick as all the time he's ever lived. It claims the window, he points at its thickness, there's this joy, all of them drawn into this density together. They're all being swept up into something that can never stop growing, it's so beautiful! There!

Roofs in the Head

It's like these layers you keep passing through, or keep trying to pass through. As if you suspect there's a ceiling somewhere, and you're going to find it soon. That's what it feels like.

You unpacked all your things. You carried them up the steep stairs from the car on the street. The computer parts were the heaviest and because the altitude is so much higher in Banff, you felt exhausted when you finished. Over and over again, up and down and up those wooden stairs. You compressed your life into a suitcase, the guitar, the computer parts and some books. You drove away from the house in Vernon, left her there in all the parts of your lives, all the angles of them back there. The softness of those parts and the way they're angled as they sit in their weight around you. The weight is what roots you to her and to yourself, too. You understand that in a depth that's rare in your life. Uprooted, anything can happen. You've always known that as well. It's the strangest quality in your life. You've wondered about it for years: that such solidity can become fluid in the snap of a finger, in the arrival of a letter, the sudden absence of a car, a new room, separate. This worries you in a way. Sometimes it's worked out well. Last year you flew down to Toronto and, apart from those two dark moments in the Bond Place Hotel, you did well. You managed not to come apart. You kept a roof over your head the whole time.

This time you're not as sure, though, and you keep glancing upwards, inside, to check the territory. There's a hint of a rift up there that just keeps going and going and you blanch in the face of it. Exhilarated, too. It's quite strange: walking up and down these stairs for a lifetime, squinting for things.

It has something to do with centres, hasn't it? All the theories point to centres, cores where everything connects. You've sought out those centres, but there are moments, aren't there, when the strength pulls in the opposite direction, when you glimpse things exploding rather than imploding, and it's terrifying and exquisite at the same time. The walls and ceilings collapse and even the slim fragile roofs you've framed and joined begin to disassemble themselves while your heart waits: to find your selves up there, splintering into everything you've ever seen or been, irrevocably separated.

Monet's Garden

It was a grand room, a thick room. It had twelve foot ceilings and high, cream-coloured walls embossed in delicate, long rectangles of polished oak. Heavy wine-coloured, velvet drapes descended like the weight of the hotel's history down the wooden window frames. Jane was leaning, her palms flat on the enamel of the window-ledge, staring down at Vernon, France, unravelling itself beneath her.

A young couple sat on a green bench in the park across from the hotel, feeding pigeons. Popcorn, Jane thought, looks like popcorn. They sat close together in front of a spray of forsythia. The young man had his free arm around his girl's shoulder, and Jane could see his hand flexing the thin porcelain line of her neck.

Jane looked up, blinked, and expanded her view so the couple sat now in the larger context of the whole green park. Geraniums and nasturtiums seared the morning light. Multi-coloured awnings, stretched taut to the shops that bordered the park on its side-streets, shone in bright greens and reds and blues, and vied with the flowers and the morning light. A shopkeeper, wearing a black beret, was hosing down the sidewalk in front of his shop, and the water there shone like silver across the flat black asphalt of the streets.

It's all like a movie, she thought, a perfect movie. Two young lovers, in a morning coda to the hymn of their bodies, hold on to one another while all around them in a bright wheel of primary colours, this French scene spins its spring idyll. She looked sideways and saw, in a room like hers in the adjacent wing of the hotel, another young couple moving around inside. They were unpacking or packing blue suitcases on a bed. Walking in and out of a white bathroom. This was a silent movie, too, and again, Jane turned away from the scene. She was watching again. How does this happen, she wondered, feeling a touch of vertigo, turning away from the window and into the room.

Jane was supposed to be having the time of her life. That's how all her friends saw this six months away. That's how she saw it herself sometimes. She sat down in the thick red chair opposite the empty bed, and stretched her legs.

Her friends in the department had thrown a wild surprise party for her before she'd left for London. She'd found four people sleeping it off on the couches and the floor the next morning. Everyone had come. Almost everyone. Sean hadn't even phoned.

Jane could see the vertical line of the window frame bisecting her head in the long mirror so the light behind her made her almost invisible, a dark object drawn into a thick chair. The cream wall to the left of her hair ran smoothly into twelve inch oak baseboards that circuited the room over the green carpet, and the chair itself swallowed her shoulders, closing her farther in. A weak light from the bathroom cast shadows over her arms and her lap, and, mixed with the generous spring light from the window, had the effect of dappling the scene, highlighting her hands while obscuring her face. She could just see her right eye catching the light while the only other break in her composure was an occasional sigh drifting like a skein of silk through the air, brushing against things.

Joyce MacLeod, the department chair, had lurched into the centre of the party and bellowed in a thick, drunken brogue, "Jane Connelly is going to take Europe by storm! Men won't know what happened to them afterwards! Three cheers for our own wandering Quixote! Three cheers for Jane the Great!" They'd all hooted and hollered, slapping her on the back, spilling drinks down her blouse. And even then, though she genuinely liked them, Jane had wondered why her friends seemed so intent on imagining some undefined salvation waiting for her in Europe, something to make things better, obviously.

She had never been to Europe before, and yet she'd spent years as a student and more as a teacher immersed in early modern writing and culture. Now, at forty, she had a feel, she thought, for turn-of-the-century *everything*: most of the events that conspired to produce modernism in England, France, Germany and Italy. At the beginning, she'd been mesmerized by the myriad connections in the flamboyant lives that fed this flowering; it seemed another, more exciting time to her. Eventually, however, she began to realize its limits, its superficialities even, and had begun to turn to her own time instead. She'd never stopped loving the Europe of these writers and artists, though, and only recently had she freed herself up to make this pilgrimage to her first love. When she'd landed at Heathrow finally, plummeting into the centre of London in a black cab, she couldn't deny that her initial enchantment for Europe had returned in a magical, almost childlike way. She'd wished then that someone she knew could have seen her excitement.

After she'd left London, she'd had an experience at The Kunstlermuseum in Basel before she'd stopped off in Strasbourg, and she thought of it now as she prepared herself for Monet. She'd gone there to see Rodin's *Burghers Of Calais.* Afterwards, she'd roamed through the permanent collection for hours. She'd gone through endless rooms of dark Renaissance, 17th and 18th century portraits when, abruptly, she'd turned into a room of French Impressionist works.

She'd almost cried for the gift of the colour. It was like walking into life itself after only emblems of what it was. The room sang with blue and red and yellow and green, and it seemed she had turned a corner and walked into the 20th century itself, into whatever had produced it, a kind of freedom and terror the earlier paintings feared. And here, in a hotel room in the landscape so dear to Monet, she felt something like the experience in Basel fusing her to her times, something in the fusion that understood and redeemed everything that was imperfect and awful and ridiculous. It seemed odd, and she laughed at how pathetic her need for this fusion was.

Jane moved her forearm into the light on the edge of the chair and observed her salmon-coloured arm and closed hand where they lay against the red velvet. She opened and closed her hand, palm up to the light. She could see the veins in the length of her arm get lost in the muted and thicker skin of her hand. She opened her palm, then closed it again.

She felt suspended somewhere in the air, between lives that were opening and closing like her hand against the velvet. What do I expect Monet will give me that the world already hasn't, and why do I do this to myself over and over again? She sighed as she remembered the good will of her friends back in Edmonton, how they'd urged her to go and have a great time. But was some of their concern out of whack, even patronizing?

She suspected some of them feared her privacy since she'd left Brian. They couldn't let it alone. They didn't seem able to understand that it nourished her. She imagined them sitting around dinner tables, clucking over her absence. Some of their concern was that simple, she thought: misguided, insecure. She knew her culture abhorred privacy, was driven to shatter it. She'd lived like that herself for a long time, surrendering to the kinetic dance of people and voices and motion. It was probably why she'd drank so much, too, and in the end, why she'd stopped.

Something was happening to her, changing. She couldn't see it clearly, and that bothered her, too. It was too big to see.

It had started before the break up with Brian, and whatever it was, it began to release her into instead of away from herself. She'd driven down to the Okanagan to visit Rick and Jennifer. She'd always had great visits with them and, typically, the way brothers and sisters do, they'd sat up late the three nights she'd been there, talking. On the first of those Rick had announced he'd quit drinking, and too many things had flickered across his face as he blurted it out.

They'd grown up like twins. From the beginning, in the small apartment that hovered over that garden in Antigonish, she and Rick had decided to figure out the world together. When they'd moved out to Edmonton just after Neil had been born, the schoolboard decided Rick should skip grade three, and the two of them entered grade four together. Day after day, they'd walked down the long gravel street to St. Agnes Elementary in the morning, a team. No matter how events conspired to separate them later, even when love claimed them in time from one another, a deep bond had been struck and had served each one of them when needed.

Rick had always been a complicated person. Nothing came easily to him. He was a boisterous, energetic man who delighted in everything, and had that kind of curiosity that ensures joy in a person's life. He was hard-working and had a unique and, to Jane at least, blessed relationship with Jennifer. But he had a self-destructive side, too.

He had drunk too much, since his early twenties. Jane had always known that. Her parents had known it. Neil had known it. But drinking was so deep in their family that none of them knew how to talk about it. Throughout their childhoods, Neil and Rick and Jane had talked about their father's helpless drinking. It had drawn them together. But confronted with it in their own adult lives, they had lost the words to discuss it, and had retreated instead into a smoothness of silence that was astonishing considering their childhoods, and their ability to still talk about it in their father. Hearing Rick speak like that suddenly, listening to him struggle with it as he sat across from her on the couch, released something silent in her, something about herself she'd tucked away so carefully she'd misplaced it.

She leaned forward into the French light suddenly, placing her forearms on her knees. Her long brown hair shuffled forward, too, and she could see one breast poking through the fabric of her housecoat where it had come loose.

"You are so soft," Sean had whispered to her one night back in Edmonton, when he still found her mysterious. He'd cupped his hand beneath her breast, lifting it to his lips. "I keep thinking I'm with this movie star, a magazine model!"

Jane stared into the flat, dark air of the room and sighed. She focused on the bouquet of roses on the table at the far side of the bed, near the door. They'd been waiting for her when she'd checked in. They were from Rick and Jennifer.

A magazine model.

She loved to drink, too, not like Rick, but more quietly. In the long run it had become something she looked forward to, a soft release from the tension that dominated her life. Most of her friends drank like her. It was part of the territory of university life: booze, cigarettes, coffee. They snuck up on you to support the sedentary nature of the work, to entertain the body while it sat for hours poring over books and articles. She'd become a professional in some ways. No one had ever seen her drunk, just boisterous, and she prided herself on her ability to measure it out carefully in this way, conceal it. Drinking carried Jane out of herself, into her relationship with Brian so she could tolerate it, and into all the hyper friendships she'd forged at work. Back then, her friends never worried about her. Back then, they knew she was happy. They looked forward to her gentle sarcasm, her manic laugh and her gift for mimicking people. So the drinking carried her away from herself and, eventually, she saw just how apt that phrase was. It completed something she'd been striving to do all her life.

She'd learned to look after everyone else. It was that simple and that complex. It was what she did.

She was nine when she realized her father would always drink like this, and her mother would always be helpless to deal with it, and so she became old enough to deal with it herself. Rick had, too. That was what had happened to them.

They were on a highway in northern Ontario in the station wagon. They were hauling a small trailer of their stuff, on their way back to Nova Scotia for a summer visit. It was the third time that morning her dad had pulled over to check the tarp on the trailor. She could hear him rustling around back there, pretending. She looked over at her mother sitting in the front seat, and realized her mother was going to pretend, too. She glanced sideways at Rick and Neil sitting in their new bathing suits, staring anxiously back at her and, suddenly, a force stronger than the beating of her heart pushed her out of the car.

He was crouched over the licence plate, taking a swig from the bottle he'd tucked under the tarp.

"Give me the bottle, Dad," she'd announced, calmly.

"What do you mean?"

"Just give it to me."

"Who do you think you are young lady?"

"Give me the bottle. You're driving. We're all depending on you, Dad. You can't do this."

"What are you talking about?"

But he handed her the bottle, and as he disappeared around the corner of the trailer muttering something about her mother, Jane walked into the ditch of horse-tail and morning glory and poured the rest of the bottle on the fine gravel that lay beneath the weeds. She walked back to the car and took her seat.

No one talked about what she'd done.

Once she'd learned a skill that big so young, she couldn't unlearn it. She'd carried it forward into everything that happened to her. She looked after Brian. She knew in her heart it was wrong, but she couldn't help it. It was too deep in her. The only thing she could do for herself was this quiet gift of drinking in the dark, a slow, innocent retreat that harmed no one. It was the only time she wasn't invisible. She'd wake up into the light of her ordinary days and become everyone she was supposed to be. It was easy.

Finally, on a low morning in February a year ago, while she was looking down on the campus from her apartment on Saskatchewan Drive, hungover, she concluded she was sick, in trouble even. She'd been drinking her way out of her own consciousness, and she realized this in a crispness, a freshness that matched the snow beneath her. So she stopped drinking, too.

It hadn't been easy at first, but she did it. The ironies were that she could pinpoint her friends' new concern for her to this exact change in her life, and it was also the point at which Brian became restless, more vocal about his miseries instead of exulting in what was happening to her, and she'd known, suddenly, that she had to leave him. It had all seemed strange.

There were wonderful aspects to the strangeness, too. Though she had to protect it from her friends, Jane had received the gift of her old, convoluted, self-defeating consciousness back. It was awful in some ways because this consciousness saw through things and into things with such a force of clarity it could terrify her. But even in this terror, her new life seemed glorified because she felt humbled by everything, aware, breathing contradictions like air. This new air was removed from the motion around her, however, and the price she paid breathing it in was a distance her friends couldn't abide. They couldn't let it alone. Finally, she decided to remove herself, go to Europe, see what might happen when she was completely by herself in it.

She could see her hands resting on her knees in the mirror. She flexed them and saw them move. She swung them back and forth and watched them swing. She leaned back into the chair again and became lost in its shadows. All she could see in the mirror were her feet now, and she wriggled her toes and watched them move, then drop out of sight onto the carpet. As she closed her eyes, she felt dizzy again, lost.

When she'd landed in London, she'd begun to feel another, more difficult distance. It had crept up on her quietly, but when it surfaced it was so real she couldn't help staring at it directly.

She'd stayed in London a week, taking advantage of an offer from Air Canada on a room in the Tavistock. As it turned out, the hotel was perfect for Jane. She was one block from Russell Square, just around the corner from Faber and Faber, two blocks from Dillon's bookstore, five blocks from the British Museum, and walking distance from all the theatres on Shaftesbury. She'd get up in the mornings, suffer the ritual hysteria of the headwaiter as he herded the hotel guests into the dining room for breakfast, then walk out into the streets looking for nothing, for everything.

On the fourth day, after a morning of feasting on Monet, Vuillard and Pissarro at the Courtauld Gallery, she'd sat and sipped a coffee at a small outdoor café in Russell Square, and everything went wrong. The world hit her full force in a way she hadn't expected. She suddenly saw herself sitting there on the old bench, childishly excited. It was as if another self, a more real self, were suspended above her somewhere and could look down on everything that was happening. This distance hit her like the weight of everything she'd ever done rolled up into one enormous package that had been dropped from the skies.

She looked at the people strolling through the park and sensed an emotion, not just in herself, but in every face she saw. It was impossible to account for such a variety of despair. It was ghastly.

A couple sat to her right on another bench beneath a gigantic elm. The woman's face was riveted to the grass while the man talked, his eyes staring into the distance of the street beyond the leaves. The woman was listening, the man explaining. It was hard to tell whether the man's audience was the woman or the distance he kept darting his nervous eyes into. In the end, the man's eyes abandoned the street and turned to the woman instead. He placed a palm upon her thigh. She removed it. It was her turn to search the distance.

It was the same everywhere Jane looked. An old man in rags bent over a garbage bin, his arms scuttling around inside. The annoyed young waiter from the café kept yelling at the old man to move on, his eyes glistening in triumph as they flicked back to his customers and imagined them pleased by his power. The customers' eyes couldn't have cared less for this small victory.

Everywhere Jane looked, there was an emptiness. Even the things around her — her blue shoes on the grass, the newspaper rustling next to her on the bench, the cars whispering by on the asphalt, the great stone buildings rising above the trees of the park — even these things had a quality, suddenly, of distance. It was as if everything had exploded in slow motion, moving endlessly but surely apart. A powerful but violent core had been destroyed, and all the fragments were hurtling outward, disconnected.

I'm one of those fragments. One of those kinetic scraps of shrapnel, torn from the centre. We surely are a mutant species. We surely are the ones in the great transition, the ones who pay the price on the front lines.

All she had seen was confusion and fear, distracted from itself by events, things and addictions, into a superficial control of the day-to-day. Beneath this illusion of control, this parade of sureness, everything was shattering outward, rescued in the end by paltry tricks of religion or idealism. In those tricks, her time was merely thrust forward, outward, into some vague design that was not part of here, was not *of this world.* She had wanted to rush out into the fragments and comfort them, say something to ease the pain. It would be ridiculous, of course, this emotional side of her that had been nurtured by her parents. She'd be arrested immediately. She'd sat there, in the midst of these distances arching over her in an awful silence, and wondered what had gone so wrong in the design.

There wasn't anything cohesive at the far end of the eyes she met. There was nothing at the base of things that could temper the fires into joy instead of destruction. It was as if a three-dimensional drama were being enacted by a two-dimensional cast. No matter how intensely the illusion worked, there was always one dimension hidden, non-existent maybe. Her own childlike joy at being here in London for the first time seemed a fragile thing with no substance behind its translucent walls.

She'd sat there most of the afternoon, blinking into the dull brass light as it faded into the red brick buildings, holding these thoughts to herself, then letting them go. How could I possibly nourish them, she'd thought. They'd destroy me. In the end, she'd returned to her room.

She was sitting in another room now, a beautiful room in an old hotel in Vernon, France, but she felt no different. Nothing had happened since London to change what she'd seen in Russell Square. She reached over for the brochures on the table in front of her chair. I might as well get on with it, she thought. Something's got to carry me out of this. Something's got to break.

She noticed the thin pile of postcards she'd filled out the night before to send back to her friends. They were all photographs of the Cathedral in Vernon, and evidence of another illusion. The postcards had buoyant messages, enthusiastic descriptions, sarcastic jokes. They were full of life and excitement. If you read them you'd wonder how anyone could be so spoiled. They flicked past her fingers like a movie about someone else. *Someone different from me,* she thought.

She thumbed the pages of the brightly coloured brochure. *Monet's Garden.* It was why she'd made the extra trip from Paris to Vernon. She'd visited Rick and Jennifer in Strasbourg and they'd made her promise to come to Vernon, stay two nights, and see Giverny where Monet had lived and painted. Rick had gone so far as to buy the return train tickets from Paris to Vernon. There was nothing she could do but go. And though she'd been carrying the weight of London in her head, Jane had grinned back at the two of them and agreed. When she'd switched trains in Paris, lurching in a cab from Gare du Nord to Gare St. Lazare, she'd felt like a sleepwalker. She'd felt a sorrow for her old joy, and wondered where it had gone.

"You look terrific!" Rick had whispered to her as he'd hugged her in the railway station in Strasbourg. "Who's the lucky guy that's caused all this?"

Her visit with Rick and Jennifer had been wonderful in some ways, but difficult in others. Rick had received a sabbatical to write and he and Jennifer had flown over to Europe to live in Strasbourg in early January. That had been another reason Jane had chosen to come to Europe.

When they picked her up at the railway station, she had to look twice. They seemed transformed to her, younger, more innocent. It was uncanny what wonders the time off had wrought. Rick was healthy, enthusiastic and open, and Jennifer looked radiant, light-hearted. They drove her to her hotel, the Hotel Gutenburg, nestled into a maze of 15th and 16th century buildings clustered around the Notre Dame Cathedral, the obvious heart of the city.

Jane hadn't expected Strasbourg to be so beautiful, so quaint. When they'd tired her out by making her walk the *quais* that circled the city, she was reminded of photographs of Venice. When they'd showed her where they lived in a small apartment in the old quarter, Petite France, Jane felt a sadness that was difficult to explain. Through their eyes, Strasbourg was a city for lovers, for romance, and in her present state of mind, Jane felt excluded. After they'd dropped her off at the hotel on the second night, she'd stood in the old window looking down on all the cafés, the cobblestone streets, the lovers whispering in the shadows, and she'd wondered what had become of her life. She had fallen asleep dreaming of her mother.

They were having lunch in the Southgate Mall in Edmonton near her parents' apartment. Jane couldn't convince her mother to treat herself. Her mother was too shy of the waiter and the elaborate offerings on the menu. She was overwhelmed by the largesse in the life Jane had grown into. She kept asking Jane about things at the university, in awe of them, savouring each detail so she could pass them on to her sisters later. In the dream Jane embellished the details because she understood what they meant to her mother. She'd wanted to reach her, tell her how much her mother's dignity meant to her. Her mother had ordered soup. It was all she could handle. Jane woke up crying out her name.

The next morning they'd gone for breakfast in a café called Koenig's near the hotel. Rick and Jennifer had joked about their lives as immigrants, spinning out hilarious stories of their difficulties with the language and the culture. Jane had watched them out of the corner of her eye. Something had happened to them over here. She'd felt pleased for them because she loved them, but there was an undertow to the ebb of their gladness, and it pulled her back into the depths of the vision she'd had in Russell Square.

When they'd dropped her off the night before, Rick had accompanied her into the hotel while Jennifer waited in the car. After they'd opened her door, as he was about to leave, Rick had given her a hug, then pulled away from her, holding onto her shoulders. "I know it's not easy sometimes," he'd whispered, staring directly into her eyes. "Believe me, I know. But don't let it weigh you down too much, or undercut everything that's happening."

"I know. I won't," Jane had whispered back at him, smiling.

His eyes had welled up suddenly and his face had shifted in emotion. He'd laughed, "It's the family curse you know! We've come by these lows naturally. There's no other way to explain them."

"I know," she'd said.

"And they're actually *good* in some ways because of where you end up."

"Where's that?"

"This time it's Giverny, my dear!"

"Why Giverny?"

"You'll see, you'll see."

"Whatever you say," and she'd given him a kiss in the doorway and watched his tall body disappear down the hall.

As she'd sat with them the next morning, sipping a bowl of *café au lait*, chatting about London, she'd become wary of their joy. She wasn't sure she should feel confident in it. She'd looked for cracks in the bright enamel, and though she couldn't find any, she suspected they were there beneath the surface. In the end, Jane had watched them standing on the platform as the train pulled away. They were holding hands. For a moment, regardless of her suspicions, Jane had wanted to believe in their love more than anything. She'd wanted to believe it was possible.

Jane stood up, removed her housecoat and had a shower. As she toweled herself off, she stood in front of the mirror fastened to the far wall on the left side of the bed. She watched herself drying her long hair, then stopped and stood, staring at her nakedness.

She thought of her parents.

Her father, Charles, would be sitting in his old green chair now, rolling a smoke, flicking through the channels for something funny. It'd be late in Edmonton. He'd have watched the CTV news with Lloyd Robertson. He'd be as bombed as he could have gotten on the extra gin he'd smuggled into the apartment earlier, past her mother's watchful eyes. He would have that ridiculous look on his face now, like he was just about to explode into his anarchic laughter. What a case he is, she smiled into the mirror.

Jane stared at her long body staring back at her. She noted the smooth curve of her shoulders, and the soft dip of her breasts. She remembered staring into them in the four-foot mirror her father had installed on the back of her bedroom door when she'd turned fourteen.

In his own quiet way, aside from the chaos, her father had paced his relationship with her by small acts of kindness like the mirror. He'd had high hopes for her. So had her mother. They wanted her to be happy in ways they felt had been denied them because of their circumstances after the war. And here she was, the product of those hopes, living in what for them could only be a fantasy. She'd written them letter after letter, measuring out the fun of the things she'd seen. She could see him sitting there nervously in the morning, before the gin, reading her adventures out to her mother with his gentle eyes taking it all in, wishing her well. Then later, after the gin, scoffing at each adventure, most pleased when something went wrong so he could laugh. *Dear old Dad,* she thought, *if you could see me now you could really laugh. You could really feel at home.*

She could see this pale, naked woman standing in front of her, framed by the oak. *That's me,* she thought. *This is it.*

She walked right up to the glass and placed her hand flat against its cool, hard surface, where her left breast was. It didn't make any difference. She was still being filmed from the outside. She thought of standing in front of Sean, and placing her hand flat against his breast.

It had all gone wrong, of course. She'd made sure it would.

She'd had an opportunity to be with someone she didn't have to save, and she hadn't known what to do. At first, because it was so purely physical, she'd simply been surprised by the pleasure he'd offered her and taken it like a gift of rain in summer.

"Like this?" she'd whispered into the corner of the pillow.

"Yes."

For the first time she could remember, Jane had wanted something for herself. She pursued it with a cunning that insured it would be driven away. She didn't know what else to do, and in some ways she wanted what lay at the far end of the pursuit: she wanted him to turn away from her. In the end, his turning away had been familiar, comfortable, and in her misery, Jane had gotten what she wanted.

She'd achieved what she'd set out to do which was disappear again. Even she couldn't explain why, but she clung to her escape like life itself. It was exactly what she needed.

She stared into the long mirror again and wondered who behind those eyes had created such havoc. At times, when she grinned a certain way and cocked her head, she could see her father playing his games; if she softened her eyes and held her head straight, she'd catch her mother smiling back at her. She noticed that one earlobe hung a bit lower than the other, that her nipples had grown erect at the memory of Sean's mouth, and her neck looked better if she swept her hair up like this, and braided it. She could see all the details in the door frame and in the room behind her reflected in the mirror, all the details except who she'd become. That wasn't clear at all. It never would be.

Enough, she sighed, and dressed to set out for the gardens. It was a five kilometer walk. She'd be there by noon.

The air in the town was humid and thick with spring. Everywhere the geraniums and nasturtiums bled against crumbling grey Normandy stone. Just before the long bridge that crossed the Seine, she said good morning to an old man who had smiled at her and doffed his black beret. He seemed the incarnation of an *entre-guerre* Frenchman. He had a neatly trimmed, thin moustache and wore a black sports coat over grey flannels. He was walking in heavy, brown boots that crumpled beneath the smoothness of the flannel. His paunch was held up by wide black suspenders. He seemed the same age as Jane's father, and he spoke English.

"You are walking to Giverny?" he stated rather than asked, a sparkle in his eye, his thick finger gesturing to the small backpack slung over Jane's shoulder. "To see my friend Claude Monet?"

Jane smiled and confessed she was.

"You will enjoy it," the man whispered melodramatically, "It is the soul of this place!" He squinted at her, then grinned. "And you are Canadian, no?"

Jane wondered how he could have guessed, then said she was.

"We have a very special place here," the man thumped his chest above his heart, "for Canadians!" His eyes welled up. Of course, Jane remembered. He meant the thousands of young Canadian soldiers who had ended up in Normandy during the war. It always amazed her how emotional the French were on this subject. And she felt grateful now. She felt a surge of pride she'd never felt before that she was the daughter of one of those soldiers.

Before they parted, the man told Jane to take the back route to Giverny. It was a wide pathway, he said, that cut through the woods and was much prettier than following the highway which was under construction. Jane smiled at the man and thanked him.

As she walked forward onto the bridge into the full sunlight, Jane felt closer to the city, the countryside, the wide grey river that shifted like history beneath the stones. At the crest of the arch of the bridge, she turned and glanced back at Vernon, its grey stone dappled beneath the green of the poplars, the spire of its cathedral breaking into a kind of song in the air, and she felt lighter, almost part of it. As she descended to the other side, she experienced a slight vertigo again, a brush of her person against the history she seemed placed down onto suddenly, but this time as if a distance were closing mercifully, and she was being gathered into something instead of being kicked out.

Nowhere in the brochures had anyone mentioned this back route to Giverny. It was a gift from the old man. She didn't meet one person in the four kilometer stretch of Lombardy poplars that lined the sides of the path. The grass in the middle was worn, but otherwise the sides were untended and wild lilacs and honeysuckles grew between the larger trees. It was a thick green corridor that seemed, almost comically, a magic entrance to something, like some scene in *Alice in Wonderland.*

Jane felt her connection to the writers and artists she'd studied come rushing up slowly like blood. It was a physical thing. Something in the combination of the old man, the honeysuckle, the poplars, this long approach to Monet, even her own despair and self-loathing, carried her into and out of herself simultaneously. She felt uneasy, but thrilled. Something was going to happen. She knew it.

Corot, Courbet, Manet, Redon, Van Gogh, Cézanne, Gauguin, Pissarro, Sisley, Vuillard and Monet. It was endless, the life they'd thrown back at her eyes. They'd all lived in this landscape and painted it a century before her. Whatever they'd seen, they'd seen it here. It was hers now.

The museum was quaint. There was a huge, mock studio that displayed full-size photographs of Monet's water-lilies series. Though it seemed tacky to be where Monet had worked and see photographs rather than originals, Jane found herself lingering over each of the vast visions anyway, soaking in their colour.

She toured Monet's house. A young American man who looked alarmingly like Sean was their guide. He was an exchange student from Boston. As he ushered them through the house, there was something about the private life of Monet, in the megalomania of the man as it surfaced through the anecdotes, that bothered Jane. She wanted to sense Monet through his landscapes. She left the house in the middle of the young man's catalogue of Monet's bright yellow kitchen, and wandered down rows of nasturtiums to a small green gate. It opened into the lower gardens where the lily ponds were. She selected a bench in the middle of it all, and sat there, shuffling her feet back and forth, waiting.

Monet had imported exotic ferns and plants from all over the world and arranged his garden so these plants shadowed the small ponds that interlaced the green. Except for patches of bright blue sky that interrupted the design occasionally, everything in Jane's field of vision shifted in endless variations of green. The ferns opposite the bench she sat on veiled the pond. The harder Jane looked, the more ferns and leaves separated her from the water that lay behind them.

She sat on the bench for most of the afternoon. She kept peering through the flowers, the vines, the bamboo, to the water sitting somewhere behind them.

Monet had arranged an ever-receding depth of vision, and had painted it over and over again. The depth only ended because of the limitations of the eye, not of the field itself. There was something at the far end of it that was always there, that offered more depth. That's what Monet had seen.

Jane was staring at herself. The depth at the far end of the field of vision was not just a physical property. Nothing could be plainer. It was *of this world.*

A young girl is swinging on a rope swing in someone's backyard. Her blonde curls stick out beneath the white cotton bonnet that is tied tightly beneath her chin. She knows her father is standing somewhere behind her, invisible, and each time she draws back up into the air, away from her mother's face grinning at her over there beneath the leaves, she can feel his hands grasp the wooden seat and give it a flick so that as she ascends now, up towards her mother, up over her mother's reaching arms, she knows she will go even higher than last time. On the trip back and up she draws in her breath until she feels her lungs will break, then pushes out the air as she glides up and over her mother's smile. This is wonderful, this pendulum swinging in the air between them. Up and back. Up and back.

She looks past the tree leaves rushing at her as she glides up again and knows this is their old backyard in Nova Scotia, before they moved out west, before the lawns and sprinklers in Edmonton. She glances down to the left on her rushing way back and sees the baby carriage and knows it is Rick in there, sleeping. This is before Neil and everything else, she thinks, and laughs as she rushes forward again into her mother's squinting grin. And though she can see through the eyes in the memory, she can also see them, bright and shiny, full of love and expectancy, gliding back and forth between her parents like this.

And, suddenly, there are roofs everywhere and she is gliding above them with the same breathless momentum of the swing. And she looks down and sees a car on a highway in the mountains. It is rounding a green bend just outside Golden after the Roger's Pass on the way to Banff, and then she is inside the car and watching a man sipping coffee from a styrofoam cup, and flicking cigarette ash into an ashtray. She can feel the man thinking. It is Rick and she can feel the rhythm of his thinking in the car as vividly as the swing pulls her up and away again and she is flying into the dark, of the streets, of the trees, of the night this time.

She looks down and sees Neil sitting on a porch in the dark, and she can feel him thinking, too, and she is gone again and this time she is swinging down over a city, and she can see all the peppered lights blinking in the dark, and the closer she gets the more she understands this is Edmonton, there's their old house down from St. Agnes, there's the cemetery hill, and there's Southgate and her parents' apartment thusting up into the air. She swings through the walls and sees her mother, her brothers and herself sitting and talking in the living room and where's Dad she wonders as she swings back up and out of this scene, and is descending into another time, another apartment, and as she swings through the walls this time she sees herself and Brian naked in the dark of a small room, making love in the night, and oh, she thinks, this is everything that is happening to me, this is everything I am in the air here between them. And she sees her mother's face beneath her again, grinning up at her, clucking out something to match the wonder she feels stretching back and forth between them here, and it seems there isn't an end to the height in either direction, nothing to stop her as her father's hands give her another flick, another push that will take her up and over into anything that might happen.

A woman walks northward in the late twentieth century, through the gate, past the poplars, back to her hotel room where the drapes are so heavy they brush the floor. She looks up into the thin clouds and remembers the smiles of her parents. Imagines their eyes in the blue up there grinning down at her. And, as she stares ahead into the long corridor of trees, she sees, at the far end of the receding band of poplars, where they converge in the almost invisible distance, her own self laughing and swinging in the green and blue air, drawing her onward, into the world.

Roofs in the Heart

Another two months down the road, and I'm back in Vernon, sitting in this small café, sorting things through.

There's endless rain this summer. It's pelting down outside the window. Men, women and children in shorts and bright beach clothes — ever hopeful — are running for cover, pulling in under any roof in the rain today.

Everything's moving, the human things I mean. Everyone's running, muscles tightening against the rain, flinching a body through it, squinting, laughing at its surprise that shouldn't be a surprise by now but still is.

In order to get at the heart, to see it, you might fracture it into its parts and examine them, then watch as they all rain down into the same music again.

Why bother getting at the heart at all? Spending these days in the head, burrowing into irony? Style? The veneer of these times? When it's all that matters in the end.

I drove around last night. I was looking for something but I didn't know what. I drove back and forth along the strip on 27th Street. Past the paint shop, Canadian Tire, Brownie's Chicken, Skipper's Seafood. Past the Husky, Chevron and Esso Self-Serves. Past the Village Green Hotel and north to Armstrong. Out on the highway, moving through the bright green fields and orchards, it was like going to Banff again. Up over the Roger's Pass, down through Golden into Field, then Banff. It felt like it for a minute. I almost believed I was driving there. But I turned around at the Kamloop's turn-off, and headed back into town, past everything again. When I pulled into the house I checked the front lawn. I do that a lot these days. I'm trying to save it. It's thin and dying. Last week I put some heavy-duty fertilizer on it. Now, I spend my time imagining it working, the grass getting thicker and greener. And even if it isn't, my eyes tell me it is. The power of the heart, to hope against the mind, that's how it works. I'm sure it's getting greener. I'm sure of it.

The voices that began in the car three months ago have stopped. They've spun themselves out, all these parts of me. A small jazz suite moves into its closing chords, picking up the disparate threads . . .

I'm running for cover under those chords, looking for a roof in their rain. Something in my heart tells me the chords are the roof. I seem to know that, but I'm flinching from their onslaught anyway.

It's all bright and green in the rain, and something's growing again.

I'm sure of it.

I can't stop smiling in the face of it, and I'm running this smile out now into the thickness of it, where there are no roofs.